GW00993224

JAGO

JAGO

BY

HAZEL M PEEL

GIETE

Copyright © H M Peel 1966
First published in 1966 by George C Harrap & Co Ltd
Reprinted 2011 by Giete
Loundshay Manor Cottage, Preston Bowyer
Milverton Somerset TA4 1QF
www.wallispeelbooks.com

Distributed by Gardners Books
1 Whittle Drive, Eastbourne, East Sussex, BN23 6QH
Tel: +44(0)1323 521555 | Fax: +44(0)1323 521666

British Library Cataloguing in Publication Data
A catalogue record for this book is available from the British Library

ISBN 978-0-9547268-9-8

Typeset by Amolibros, Milverton, Somerset
This book production has been managed by Amolibros
Printed and bound by T J International Ltd, Padstow, Cornwall, UK

Contents

Illustrations

TO MY HUSBAND

I give JAGO as
a companion to FURY

With flowing tail and flying mane,
Wide nostrils never stretch'd by pain,
Mouths bloodless to the bit or rein,
And feet that iron never shod,
And flanks unscarr'd by spur or rod,
A thousand horse—the wild—the free,
Like waves that follow o'er the sea,
Came thickly thundering on.

(Lord Byron—"Mazeppa")

CHAPTER ONE

The Race

THE horse was red, a true red. Not the chestnut of England, nor even the sorrel of America, but almost the bright red of the poinsettia leaf under the noonday sun. In the crowded heat of the paddock Peter Huston allowed himself yet once more to admire the beauty of his horse. The head was small and well bred with small ears topping widely-spaced eyes, and a concave nose running down to flared, almost Arabian, nostrils. The neck was arched and iron muscles swooped down to disappear into long, sloping shoulders. The girth was deep with a large rib cage, the back short and firm. From the quarters the tail cascaded down in a red river of glowing hair to tumble round the wide hocks in a profusion of colour. The four legs stood rock firm on dainty feet, the tendons standing out and almost cutting into the skin like cords of steel. The cannon bones slid into neat fetlock joints where white hair plummeted into light-coloured hooves. It was almost as if the horse had stepped no more than fetlock-deep into a pool of white paint.

Around the paddock rails the spectators stared at the red colt in deepest interest. Few, if any, would have guessed that behind the composed face of the trainer was a mind whirling with worry and apprehension. In all the flat race meetings he had attended in his forty years of life, Peter Huston had never been in quite this state of concern. And all over a horse!

With the jockey he started to walk across to where the groom had at last persuaded the red colt to plod beside him in a sedate circle round the paddock. The trainer stopped and looked anxiously at the jockey then threw another glance at his horse. He noted the signs of rising temper, the rolling eyes, the skin twitching as nerves began to jump. Already the colt's steps were becoming short and snappy. He ducked his head to snap at the bit and grind on the metal, and flailed his tail in warning as he tested the groom's strength on the reins. None of this escaped Peter Huston and he groaned inwardly.

"He's as tensed up as any bush ranger at his first bail-up!" he said.

The jockey needed no telling. With apprehensive eyes he watched the groom lead the red colt towards them.

"This is his last chance," said Peter Huston. "Try not to get thrown. If someone could only stay with him we might get somewhere but if he makes a fool of me again then out he goes. Sold for whatever I can get!"

Trainer, jockey and groom prepared warily. They had to get the jockey on to the saddle and then it was up to him to try and stay there.

The red colt knew it all. The girth would be tightened, the stirrups lowered, the man's hands would grasp the rein and the weight would crouch in the saddle. He would be ordered, bullied and if necessary punished into absolute obedience; to run and gallop and race for the man on his back.

He reared high, screeching his protest, trying to snap the reins out of the groom's hand. The reins jerked, pulling on the snaffle bit, and this sudden pain changed the colt's emotions from objection to angry temper.

He pulled farther away from the men, straining back on his hocks, his front feet stamping on the ground, his head high, tugging at the reins, hurting his mouth. He whipped his head aside, at the same time rearing high in an effort to dodge the men. They clustered around him, wary of his feet but still clinging to the reins.

Even the red colt could not stay rearing for ever. As he dropped down the men seized him. The reins were shortened until the bit gripped his jaw, large hands clamped down on his nostrils, cutting off his breathing, and panic-stricken he stood still, flanks heaving, sweat darkening his red coat to a dull black.

He saw the jockey preparing to mount but he could not fight without air. He flinched as the man's weight landed on his back, strained as the bit moved in his mouth, then the pressure went from his nostrils and he was free to fight again.

For the second time he reared, front feet dangling awkwardly, but the jockey rapped the top of his head. The sudden shock brought the colt down. He dropped, stiffening his legs preparatory to bucking, but the bit pulled against the corners of his mouth, instructions from the jockey's boots drummed into his flanks, and reluctantly the red colt moved into a trot out of the paddock. Every instinct wanted to fight, every muscle was being controlled by the man so that fight was impossible.

All the way down to the starting post the colt was wanting to remove the man but the opportunity to empty his saddle didn't come. The jockey was too shrewd, too strong and too alert. Every snatch at the bit was restrained, every potential swerve and kick was halted with orders from the legs.

But as they neared the milling line of excitable horses, the cursing jockeys, the general hubbub, the colt sensed the sudden distraction of the man on his back. Without thought, moving only as an uncoiled spring, he turned. He propped sharply to the left, his four legs drumming on the ground in rhythm, stiff as iron, their concerted movements painfully jarring to the jockey. One more violent, bone-snapping prop in the other direction and the red colt felt the man's weight move in the saddle.

Greatly encouraged, he half reared then plunged forward into the air, crashing down on the sun-bleached turf, legs as stiff as wood stakes. This final jolt was too much for the jockey. His eyes blurred, his neck jerked and he had to let go.

The colt assisted him further by spinning around on his hocks and plunging in the opposite direction. He felt his saddle empty and darted forward away from the line of wildly excited racehorses. The tiny stirrups clanged against the saddle flaps, the reins dangled loosely on his neck. He pushed himself into a canter and happily moved away from all men. At the bottom end of the rails he slowed down, turned, and watched.

The jockey scrambled to his feet, shaken and angry, and walked back to the horse. The colt watched his approach, torn between fresh emotions. He had no dislike of the man on foot but he knew that when the reins were caught again, when the bit ordered in his mouth, other men would come, and once again the weight would thump on to his back.

The red colt passaged sideways, away from the approaching jockey, keeping a set distance between them. His head was high, the ears pricked forward alertly, the nostrils flaring as they took in the man's scent. He backed away again until he felt the rails against his quarters, then fear took over—the fear of any animal at being trapped.

There were men everywhere. Men on the rails, hooting, laughing, and shouting. Men approaching him from the front, men nearing his flanks, everywhere men came forward to catch him.

The colt reared again, screeching his defiance, then flattening his ears he shot forward into a wild canter for freedom. He saw one man leap for the reins but twisting he evaded him, then another man was in his path and a whip cracked in his face. The unexpected sound unnerved him. He halted, dithering uncertainly, not wanting to strike and hurt but afraid of being caught.

His hesitation was his undoing. He felt the tearing pain in his mouth as the reins were seized. Hands pulled his head down, clamping on his nostrils, holding his ears, and though he struggled furiously, intent now on kicking his way to freedom, he had no chance with his head restrained.

He felt the jockey flop into his saddle again, his head was released, and the bit worked on his gums and mouth corners. Heels dug into his flanks and the small whip bit into his shoulder.

In reluctant obedience he shot forward to line up again, his whole being shaking with resentment.

The Starter saw he had them, signalled, and they were off—a rippling line of colourful thoroughbreds racing under the Queensland sun, the turf short and brown from lack of water, the going hard and straight. The crowd roared its approval at this delayed start, not too dissatisfied owing to the unexpected entertainment from the red colt.

The colt ran mulishly, not really trying, only concerned with the man on his back. This he paid for with another bite from the whip. Sullenly he increased his pace to avoid more pain but the tide of his emotions was rising too quickly now. The surf of anger was boring forward, churning with the rollers of resentment, and the colt broke stride, changing his legs, shaking the jockey's rhythm. Rapidly they dropped to the end of the field.

If the jockey had tried to coax the colt forward all might still have been well. But the jockey was raging. He had been humiliated before his colleagues, he too burned with resentment, and lifting his switch he cut sharply into the colt's right flank.

The colt shuddered at the pain, automatically veering to the left and away from it. Totally unprepared, the jockey swayed, his knee-grip loosening, the reins slackening as he waved his hands for balance.

The colt felt it all and being an intelligent animal seized his opportunity. He plunged again to the left, ducked his head, arched his back and kicked both hind legs into the air. He was almost vertical when he felt the saddle empty and with another bound of exultation he kicked again, straightened, cantered briskly away from the jockey, and joyfully chased after the field.

Like all horses, he wanted to catch up with his racing companions and he drummed his feet on the hard ground as he thrust into a gallop. Red tail flying, mane bouncing, legs stretching, he flowed over the ground in long, seemingly effortless, strides. His large body had ample room for expansion of heart and lungs and the nostrils dilated for extra air; his dainty feet only flicked the ground and already he was cutting down the distance. He drew level with the last horse and floating on with great strides he blithely passed the field, one horse after another.

The jockeys cursed him, driving him away from their path with shouts, so he galloped even faster and finally took the lead, red tail waving cheekily in their faces.

He passed the winning post but riderless he saw no reason to stop, so wildly he continued his own race, only faltering when

He cantered away from the jockey and chased after the field.

he realized his solitary state. Halting at last, the red colt stood with flanks heaving, certainly not unduly distressed though the sweat streamed down his blazing coat, plopping on to the dust in little dabs of salty moisture.

Alone but satisfied, the colt lowered his head and snapped his teeth at the stunted and savourless grass. Never before had he won such a battle.

They came to catch him and clear the track for the next race —three men on foot and two mounted with ropes.

Although wary enough to dodge the men on foot the colt knew nothing about the peril from a mounted man. He made no attempt to keep away from the ridden horses, he even crowded them at one stage, pressing instinctively for protection against the walking men as he swung his head to keep the trailing reins free.

But the young colt learned a quick lesson. Ropes circled his neck, schooled horses keeping them taut, and he was a helpless prisoner. On each side a rope was wound around a saddle pommel, and when the colt lunged for his freedom, the ropes bit into his neck. He could not turn, he could go neither forward nor backward. Ignominiously he was led away, a rider and a rope on each side.

The red colt strained until the ropes scored his flesh but he soon realized the uselessness of resistance. Being intelligent and quick, however, his brain had already registered the fact that mounted men meant pain and imprisonment. Another bitter fact was stored away: that horses of riders were not friends who would aid and abet; they only acted upon the men's orders. To fly to them for safety meant falling back into the clutches of man, being a prisoner, and undergoing the indignity of a rider on one's back. The thrown jockey had proved one thing, however, that man was not inviolable, he could be beaten. Very slowly it had begun to penetrate the colt's brain that man was not all-powerful.

As the red colt trotted mutinously back, fettered with the cutting ropes, his emotions were as mixed as the dust his feet stirred up. He did not think about the future, he could not reason, all he knew was that freedom was precious. To be without the rider was sublime bliss, to walk, trot, canter, and gallop exactly as he pleased was the ultimate in living.

He trotted parallel with the ropes now, not fighting them and so avoiding pain. This lesson he would never forget: ropes mean pain, avoid them when you can. If caught, do not resist them. Wait, watch, be ready when the opportunity comes, for come it will and only he who seizes it deserves to succeed.

CHAPTER TWO

Jago

"WELL, there's your cheque!"
"And he's cheap at the price. When I think of that breeding—!" Peter Huston shook his head at the heartbreak the red colt had given him. Bred so carefully, raised so patiently, and now at three years useless for the racecourse and labelled unrideable. "I hope you have better luck with him. He'd have made a bonza stud after he'd finished racing," he continued, eyeing the horse in gloom.

Mike Colston grinned as he rubbed his hands together. "We'll straighten him out. I've got an abo back home who can ride the pants off anything with four legs. Get a good stock saddle on him, and my Warrigan, and that horse'll soon come to his senses. What do you call him, anyhow?"

"Jago!"

"Queer name for a horse!"

"I combined the names of his sire and his dam when he was born. He's by Go-along out of Jaqueena but I thought Jago sounded better than Goja! I've a few other names for him right now!"

"Never mind, sport! He's not your worry now. You've cut your losses, you can try again. I'll let you know when we're collecting him."

Peter Huston did not reply. He was staring regretfully at a small, railed yard. Inside stood Jago, the big red colt whom he was about to lose. He had bred, trained and raced many horses but never one with such good looks as these. Jago was a giant among his contemporaries. He recalled breeding the colt's sire and dam with infinite care and only after much study of their respective bloodlines. He had been delighted when the gangly-legged foal had entered the world because, like all horsemen, he wanted to own the perfect horse; and, more practically, he wanted a top-class racehorse capable of entering for the best races.

Somewhere, however, Peter Huston knew that he had erred. The red colt was beautiful beyond words, the red legs had proved that they could outstrip all others, but somewhere in that awesome pedigree a stream of rebel blood had poured forth, mixing, coursing, and never diluting until in the big red colt it had burst into a fiery river, in outright revolt against being saddled and ridden by man. In Jago there was more than the normal spark of rebellion against man—there was a touch of the outlaw, even the finger of the rogue.

The trainer scowled. No horse had ever beaten him. He was considered an authority on the breeding and training of the very best types of racehorse. The red colt was going to be the absolute ultimate in winners—until he came to back him.

It was then he had found out that his marvellous red horse hated the saddle and resisted a man on his back with all the force at his command. In vain had he battled, fought, cursed, and to a certain extent insisted on his own way. The red colt retaliated by refusing to win even one humble race.

But now Huston had made up his mind once and for all. He could not go on battling with such an animal . . .

"I'll let you know when we're collecting him," repeated Mike Colston, jerking the trainer abruptly away from his bitter thoughts.

•

Jago knew the two men were discussing him. All his life he had been aware of the sound of the human voice. As soon as he had become old enough to understand things like the sun and the grass, the wind and the dust, he had learned about the sounds men made.

Their voices had different tones, deep for the men, lighter for women, and a shrill piping from children. He learned too to recognize the quiet, soft, rippling note which came with pleasure and approval. This was usually accompanied by a pat on the neck, a rub around the nose, and an affectionate pull of his small ears. Then there was the negative tone which Jago had understood meant nothing to him. It was the flat note which men used when communicating between themselves. Finally there was the harsh sound when men's voices deepened, when the growl came into their throats, when anger was shown. With this Jago connected pain from the bit or spurs or stick. He soon understood which actions of his would bring about this angry note and learned to avoid such actions.

He even isolated special words which when uttered in the negative tone were easily understood: "Stand" and "Whoa", "Now then" and "Back"—short, crisp words which went with certain movements. As he was above average intelligence for his species, it is possible that in time he could have been trained to understand short, simple sentences and with the help of significant gestures from a man's hand could have performed as adequately as any circus horse.

Jago knew now that he was the subject of the two men's talk. They were using only the flat, dull negative tone but their eyes were on him continually and even without this he would have sensed their interest. Like all animals he was highly conscious of the human eye. A long stare disconcerted him, distracted his attention from the matter in hand, and made him either curious or nervous, the two emotions depending upon the tone of the voice, the gesture of the hand.

The hand of a man was important. Jago learned this as a foal. There was something magnetic about the sleek smoothness of a man's palm when it travelled the length of his head, tousled his ears or slapped his neck, a feeling akin to the sensitive nudge from his dam's nose or lips.

As man uses his hands so do horses use their lips. Touching, feeling, and ascertaining whether friend or foe, good or bad, hot or cold. Jago crowded the rails and slowly extending his head ran his lips over the nearest man while his nostrils dilated absorbing the strange scent.

Mike Colston put his hand on the colt's nose and rubbed briskly, drinking in the horse's physical perfection, while his eyes ran over the splendid body and fiery coat.

He was a big man. Big in height and weight, speech and action. As big and harsh as the country on which he lived. Middle-aged now, he had a brown face laced with lines around the eyes which were narrowed by years of screwing themselves up against the glare of the sun. He didn't stand so much as straddle the ground, legs apart, feet at an angle, as if bracing himself against the elements.

He was a cattle man, running good beef steers from his Queensland station, battling in continual succession with the weather, the beef market, the kangaroos, and the frustrating perplexity when his aborigine boys packed up for their inexplicable walkabouts. He had seen lean years, when only his own guts had kept him going; dry hot years when his stock died by the hundred from thirst, when hot winds attacked the land, killing off the already poor grass and leaving just a brown smear on the earth. He had seen the water holes dry up until the earth cracked in a gigantic mosaic, and until the only decoration around these weird crazy-paving stretches of earth, was the sun-bleached skeletons of his stock.

He had fought the land, cursed the weather, slogged to find water and sink bores, working himself to a lean wraith of the former man, but he had never quit. His type does not know the word. And after the lean years came the good when the rains fell at their appointed time, and the grass grew again; not thick, lush, green grass but a stringy variety, poorish and sparse but enough to keep stock alive. With the rains came the sudden upsurge in the price of beef, when the markets were fantastically good and money suddenly became a commonplace commodity.

Himself from shrewd Scottish stock, Mike Colston carefully ploughed back much of the money on to his property, mostly drilling bore holes and finding precious water for when the lean years came again.

He had little time to play but he managed to marry and raise two children, and suddenly one day he found himself to be middle-aged and rich. He decided to buy a horse, one good enough to run in the bush races which the outback people so adored. He had no pretensions to try to win the Melbourne Cup, he just wanted a horse well bred enough to race and give him a hobby.

Of course he knew about Jago's quirk but this did not perturb him. In the outback, they had their own way of going about breaking and riding a horse; he knew in his own mind that either he himself, or his best aborigine rider could stick on the red colt. What could southern racing people hope to achieve with their smaller racing saddles?

He knew he was lucky to get such a well-bred animal so cheaply, and satisfied, he rubbed Jago's nose again. The red colt had a lot of learning coming his way, too right he had!

The colt sensed the strength of the man from his contact with lips and hand. This man looked different and smelt different. He had a slower speech, his movements were more clumsy but he was all male and he was strong. Any animal recognizes this.

After the men had gone, Jago walked idly around his small paddock, not thinking as a man would, but listening, and absorbing sounds and scents picked up with ears and nostrils.

Since the disastrous race he had been flown back to the place of his birth, Peter Huston's stud in Victoria. Jago had lived there all his life; apart from the racecourses, he had no experience of other places. He knew the various buildings and could identify them by their scent. The feed room smelled of oats and bran and processed foods. The hated saddles were kept in another building which smelled of leather. His dam and the other mares lived in a far paddock, out of sight but still within communication. Then there were the powerful and awe-inspiring scents from the three standing stallions, great brutes of horses who flaunted themselves arrogantly and had aroused the foal's first feeling of fright. This had quickly turned to wonder and curiosity and now Jago felt something akin to these horses though as yet he had no knowledge of what this was. All he yet knew was that if the stallions ran loose and he were free, he would step back, acknowledging his inferiority.

He knew Victorian weather which could run to extremes of temperature; the boiling heat of the day and the bitter cold of the winter nights were common at the stud's high altitude. He did not know snow or ice as an English thoroughbred would, though in the great heart of Australia there are mountain ranges where the snow fluffs down under the winter wind.

All Jago knew was this homeland where every whisper of scent and sound meant something with which he could associate some fact or other, whether animal, human or weather.

Jago had no knowledge that he had changed owners. A dog would perhaps have known this instinctively but a dog lives in closer communion with man in his home. He has more time to observe and connect actions and moods; he is also a very good guesser.

If Jago had known he would not have cared. A horse is more aloof and self-sufficient than a dog, more like a cat. One owner is nearly as good as another. As long as food and water were there, the red colt considered little else.

There were other feelings and instincts in Jago which had not even started to move; though only surface deep they were still dormant and because of this the men had no trouble with him. He had a long way to travel to the Queensland station and strange men were to handle him, but from birth Jago had been used to travelling in various ways. By truck or plane he was happy enough to step into the conveyance, to be tied and fed while he was moved from one place to another. There was nothing alarming in something so normal; without a backward glance or whinny Jago left his birthplace to travel north by truck and plane and truck again. In a way, he even enjoyed the journey. Food and water were there under his nose and when they were gone fresh food appeared. To his mind this was one of the most remarkable things about man—his endless ability to provide food and water; not just grass or hay but the more tasty dried foods and that absolute delicacy in the shape of oats.

In Jago's brief life he had met nothing of importance that was not in some way connected with man. He could not even consider a life without man, which was perfectly reasonable considering that he was a true, domesticated animal. His whole world was narrow and limited and when he eventually arrived at his destination he walked calmly from the truck and allowed himself to be turned into another small, railed paddock.

It was not until night that Jago became aware of the subtle difference of his new home. There were so many things to look at, so many strange scents and smells on the breeze, that he spent the whole night just standing and sniffing and listening.

To start with, the station had its own peculiar smell. It was harsh and very dry, and a fine dust, almost invisible to the eye, was continually in the air. This dust carried the strange smells: the scents of the wild outback, the unknown bush. There were animal smells and plant smells, dust and earth smells, none of which had any catalogued compartment in Jago's brain because he had never met them before. He was as much a stranger in the outback as man is in the sea. He was not a creature of this land or life. He had to learn everything in the air and on the ground and even under the ground. Every tiny smell had to be tracked down, accounted for, identified for good or evil, then stored away until wanted.

It was the same with the sounds. The big white man had different-sounding footsteps, heavy and slow but sure and firm. His weatherboard house, standing on concrete stumps against the ants, creaked with dryness, groaned in the night, and talked afresh at dawn. Every plank and beam made its own distinctive sound.

Then there were the entrancing sounds of the station itself. Sounds from men. White men and strange black men. Men who had a harsh, acrid smell, who looked different, whose speech and movements were unknown to the colt.

Away in the distance, carried to him on the breeze, came the mournful sounds of the beef cattle and the tiny fluttering noises from the arms of the windmills which worked the bores for water. He heard too the odd rattles from the large, galvanized iron water tanks which were placed around the wooden house, catching the water from the roof when it rained, storing it for use.

Everything was alien and at the same time exciting. There was even something about the breeze itself. Jago stood, his head high and his nostrils flaring, tense and quivering. The breeze was exciting beyond thought but the reason escaped him as yet. The wind which had travelled over the great dry land for hundreds of miles brought more than just strange scents and sounds. It brought something which roused the first stirrings of his ancestors in his blood. Long, long ago, before men and thought and almost before time itself, Jago's ancestors had roamed free and wild, unfettered and untroubled by man. The true wild horse owed allegiance to no man, nor animal. He roamed and fought, mated and reproduced, and when the cycle ended, quietly died. He knew no form of restraint beyond the acknowledged orders of hunger, thirst, and herd rule from the stallion. This tickle of instinct, this faint stirring in his blood, was sufficient to unsettle Jago. He did not yet know what it was, he could not understand this new thing, he only knew it was so; that when the breezes blew they brought more than smells, they charged emotions which were inexplicable but nevertheless explosive.

Although a domesticated animal from centuries of selective breeding, the red colt was experiencing the first unsettled pangs which even civilized man understands when he leaves his crowded cities and stands on a lonely, windswept, sun-bleached beach and stares mesmerized at a seething white-and-blue-capped ocean. From those depths came his ancestors, and in all man, even the most polished and urbane, arises the same puzzling tug of wild exultation when the salt winds beat on his city-pallid face, when the heart spurts and the blood races.

Jago roamed his paddock that night, too pent-up and torn by these new feelings, too overwhelmed by all this vast strangeness to settle and eat the feed which had been tossed to him.

The dawn slipped over the sky with the sun blazing from the horizon, already a fiery ball of heat, and the station creaked to life again. With it came more things to see, sounds to hear, and smells to assimilate.

The dogs came first, querulous and growling, with raised hackles and lolling tongues. Then came the people, white and black, Mike Colston's wife and children as sun-tanned and tough as himself. The black people walked slowly, not proudly but almost lazily, and only one was different.

He was a large aborigine, nearly as tall as the white man, with thick shoulders and long, well-muscled thighs. Dressed in a multi-coloured shirt, faded blue jeans and dark high-heeled boots, he stood square and firm, his crinkled black face eyeing the red colt. The whites of the man's eyes stood out in sharp contrast to the colour of his skin. Between thickened nose and lips and wavy hair, sharp eyes bored into the colt.

Jago backed a step, uneasy under this stare, worried by this fresh man-scent so different from that which he had always known. The black man stood immobile, only his eyes moving, and the colt stared back at him, his nostrils absorbing the alien scent.

Like so many of his race, Warrigan was a superb horseman with great balance and tremendous grip. One of the things which had so astounded the early white settlers was the ease with which the aborigine had taken to the strange horse. They had natural riding ability and Warrigan was a priceless advertisement of this. As chief black stockman he was Mike Colston's right hand. He was a first-class tracker, a brilliant cattle man and above all he only rarely now succumbed to the walkabout urge—that queer feeling which makes the aborigine stop whatever he is doing and go bush for weeks at a time, suddenly to reappear without warning and pick up his job almost where he had left it weeks before.

He was a full blood, as was his gin, and they lived on one of the better wooden houses on the station. His schooling had been limited; the wild young abo boy took little interest in the printed word. Instead he had been content to wander and follow the stockmen around, watching, observing, and listening, combining this store of white man's knowledge and doings with his own priceless black man's knowledge of the Australian outback.

Mike Colston had absolute faith that his black Warrigan could turn the unrideable red colt into a successful bush racer, and with an ordinary horse this might have been so.

But Jago was not ordinary. He was the unlikely throwback, the natural rebel, and already the first stirrings of the wild had quickened his blood. He was the classically bred horse with lightning-fast reactions, with an above-average intelligence, with a rock-hard determination that no man should stay on his back.

To give Warrigan credit he was a good horseman but he in his turn had never before met a pure, aristocratic thoroughbred.

All the black man's experience had come from the broken brumbies and half-bred horses sired by the station stallion.

He was totally unsuited to handle such a highly strung and well-bred animal as the red colt, as unsuited as the pick and shovel labourer would be in trying to use his hard, calloused hands on the delicate fingerwork of watch repairing.

What was to follow was as inevitable as night following day.

CHAPTER THREE

The Fight

COMPARED to other stations Bereeba was large and had become prosperous. The land ran in a mixture of open bush, running flat and hilly, and thickish scrub spattered with gum trees. A lot had been ring-barked and looked ghostly white in the moonlight; during the day they were naked and rather forlorn under the sun.

The soil was neither particularly good nor bad but it did produce grass to run the stock. To a newcomer the land appeared harsh, brown, and totally burned up by the sun when sometimes during the day heat-waves shimmered in dancing lines and even mirages would appear.

The station house had been sensibly built near water, a small river which in dry weather sometimes failed and in wet weather was liable to become a raging torrent. Around the house and outbuildings the land had been cleared toe-high, nothing being left that could aid a bush fire. All the tall grass was kept cut down, the trees were not allowed to grow, and the firebreak was never neglected.

As in most outback stations the Colstons were connected with their neighbours by radio, and every morning and evening, at set times, either man or wife would sit down, tune in, and listen to the news, telegrams, and other personal messages which flashed through the ether. At times their harsh life was intensified when the flying doctor was called and every outback housewife was as capable as the doctor at breaking serum capsules and injecting anti-snake serum into a leg far too often bitten. But they were happy and self-sufficient people. Every so often they had their fun at the bush races when friends and neighbours arrived from a distance of a hundred miles or more to race horses, to make outlandish bets, and to drink far more beer than was good for them.

It was to these tough, hard, happy people that Jago had been brought. As they worked hard and lived hard, so did they play. Most stations had their aborigines who lived and worked where they were born. These were not reserve abos but almost family ones, the sick children and gins being doctored by the station wives, the boys and bucks growing up and working with the station men.

Bereeba was a good station. Black and white mixed and worked together amicably because the Colstons, being fourth-generations Scottish settlers, were as steeped in the aboriginal customs as the abos themselves. They understood them—which made it all the more astonishing that Mike Colston let Warrigan handle Jago.

The large buck had no idea of the finesse and skill required in handling a temperamental and highly strung thoroughbred horse. Strong arm and rough methods worked wonders with the brumbies but to use them on the aristocratic red colt was courting trouble.

The black man and the colt started off well enough but this could never last.

"Watch your step with him! He's had all his own way so far. I want him sorted out but don't get too rough," warned Mike Colston.

"Sure, boss! I sort him out, too right I will!"

Satisfied, Mike Colston left Jago to Warrigan. This was a bad mistake.

Warrigan decided to work the colt in the late afternoon when some of the heat had gone, but first he had to saddle him and before that catch him. So he did the natural thing, he fetched a rope.

Jago had stood happily all day in the paddock, drinking in this vast, strange, sun-burnt land which was so different from anything else he had known. He had become slightly more used to the black man's peculiar scent during the day as he worked around the homestead and he was not unduly alarmed when he came into the small paddock.

Jago turned and faced him, head high, ears pricked forward in curiosity. The man spoke in the negative tone and the colt was just debating whether an approach would produce a sugar lump or other tit-bit when his eyes noted something else—the coiled rope hanging in the man's hand at his side.

The sight of the rope, although coiled and still, was enough to trigger off a memory reaction in his intelligent brain. Ropes meant capture, and loss of freedom meant saddles, which in turn, pointed to someone on his back.

Jago stood still, seeing the danger, not knowing quite how to avoid it. The paddock was small, the railed fences were too high to jump, so nervously he backed away placing his body at an extreme distance to the man.

Jago watched with growing nervousness as the man swung the rope free, twirled it and spun it through the air. It moved quickly, almost too quick for sight, but the red colt was even quicker. His instincts prodded his lightning muscles to action and he shot sideways, away from the looped rope which flopped on the ground.

Thoroughly alert and afraid now at the intended capture Jago raced around the small paddock, frantically trying to outpace the rope while the man stood quietly in the centre and waited his chance.

The rope flew again, hovered and dropped neatly around the colt's neck. It tightened and Jago burst into frenzied panic as pain caught at his windpipe, cutting off his breath, choking him. He reared high, remembering too late that such a movement with a rope meant increased pain. Dropping down he tried to evade the rope, twisting first to right then left, but the man played him in skilful fishing sweeps, always keeping an even distance and tautness.

Finally Jago halted and stood at the extreme end of the rope, eyeing the man, alert for the slightest movement which he could evade. He felt sore and hurt around his neck and, moving his head an inch, he felt the rope slacken, the biting pain decrease.

He experimented again and found that by giving to the rope, much of the hurt vanished. This meant advancing a step nearer to the man, which was contrary to his present feeling, but the relief from pain overcame the emotion.

Jago stared hard at the man, wondering what was going to happen next, how soon a saddle would be put on his back. He saw the rope snubbed around a post and he watched as the man walked away, then his unease increased as the man came back with saddle and bridle in his arms. The smell of leather hit his nostrils and instinctively Jago backed a step only to feel again the cutting of the rope. With great reluctance he stepped forward, his eyes never leaving the man, his ears flickering in fright and uncertainty.

The man placed the saddle on the hard ground, drew a scarf from his jeans pocket and slowly approached the red colt, talking softly in his tribal tongue.

Jago flinched as the man approached but stood his ground.

As yet the man had done nothing to make him attack, and in fact this thought had not occurred to the colt so he simply stood unhappily while a large hand ran down his neck, then slid over his nose.

In one quick movement his eyes were covered with a blindfold. Jago stood in utter horror as his sight vanished. He had never considered anything quite so terrible. He dare not move, he could not move, and he started to shudder in fear and panic. The humiliation was nothing compared to the fright, and this in its turn was nothing to the betrayal he felt when the saddle clumped on to his back.

He squirmed, blew out, but otherwise stood shaking while the girth was drawn up under his belly and fastened.

The Australian stock saddle is entirely different from a racing saddle or even a standard hunting saddle. It is strong and heavy with a deep seat, high pommel and cantle, and thick knee-rolls. It is a saddle for use all day and if necessary all night. It is supremely comfortable, difficult to fall out of, and perfectly balanced. The stirrup leathers fasten at the bottom, near the iron, as opposed to the English saddle where the leathers fasten high up under the small saddle skirt. As the American cowboy's saddle is superior for long-distance riding and comfort to the standard hunting saddle, so the Australian stockman's is a sheer dream for riding compared to almost any other saddle. It is, however, very heavy.

Jago had only ever been ridden with the lightweight, forward-cut racing saddle; he had never even had a heavy weight on his back; and he squirmed again at the heavy load as it was tightly girthed into place.

What terrible thing was this on his back? He had never been so shocked and horrified in all his short life. Large hands grasped his mouth, forcing the bit into place and the headpiece was roughly dragged over his ears and fastened under his throat. He trembled again, too frightened to fight.

He felt the reins over his neck, the squeeze of the girth being tightened another hole, and then a hand grasped his nostrils and he could not breathe. The blindfold was whipped from his head and, blessèd relief, he could see again, but now he could not breathe, and how his nose hurt under the cruel pinch.

Jago stood, rolled his eyes and waited for fresh horrors. He saw the black rider preparing to mount and suddenly the pinch on his nostrils increased, his neck was swung round acutely and in one smooth movement, the rider had vaulted into the saddle, and Jago's head was free.

He stood still, gulping in the air, too appalled to do anything at all. He felt the bit lifting his head, and a vicious pain shot through his flanks as the rider's spurs bit. He jumped forward a step, trying to sort all this out in his mind, shocked again by the pain from the spurs, sharp, rowelled, bushman's spurs.

The spurs bit flesh for a second time and Jago again shot forward and halted. Why was this happening? Why did this man hurt him so much? Pain only came as punishment; he had done no wrong, the man was on his back, so why was he hurting him?

Jago was not to realize just yet that the rider was needling him into a fight so that he could outride him.

Another searing pain tore into his ribs and Jago's mood began to alter. He was too proud ever to be browbeaten and now his natural instincts as a fighter were rising, not so much against the man on his back, but against the pain the man was inflicting on him.

A fourth time the spurs raked, leaving bloody lines, and at

this point Jago exploded. He shot forward, head ducked, back arched, and kicked to right and left, expecting the saddle to empty, waiting for the rider to fall like the jockey. For his pains he only received another slash from the spurs. This was sufficient really to enrage him.

He began to fight in earnest. His back curved into the air as with four straight legs he flung himself into a series of wild bucks. His nose was almost scraping the dust, his tail was clamped down like a vice against his thighs, and every muscle was straining in effort.

Again and yet again the spurs cut, sending Jago berserk. He flung himself about in a fantastic series of leaps, bucks, kicks, and plunges that jarred even his own body. But the rider stuck like glue. Such antics were quite normal to Warrigan.

The black man rode deep in the saddle, his seat not lifting from the leather. His thigh muscles bulged through his jeans as they took the strain from the violent plunges, his elbows were clamped against his ribs, and he stared straight ahead, neck rigid, every sense alert. A wild gleam lit his eyes, a slightly sadistic smile creasing his black face. It never entered his head that a gentler approach without the spurs would have produced better results.

Jago flung himself around at the paddock's end, rearing then hurtling through the air in a fly-jump, landing with iron legs drumming up a cloud of dust which clung to his sweating belly. He propped to the right, veered to the left, changed directions in mid-air, switched from bucks to rears then back to bucks again, and still his rider didn't move one inch.

Jago was breathing heavily now, his red coat dripping sweat on to the ground; his eyes were wild with temper and frustration, his heart crashed against his ribs, but still the man stuck.

Now his intelligent brain started to work. He had been through his whole repertoire without result, he must try something different. He charged at the railed fence and flung his body heavily against the posts, but he only hurt himself. The canny rider knew that move and had shifted his leg in time.

Jago grunted with the fresh pain and screeched as the spurs bit again, finding fresh strength as rage flowed. This was no game now but a live or die battle.

He crossed the paddock again, plunging up and down, never still for one second, his body either horizontal in fly-jumps or vertical in kicks, and these movements interspersed with bucks, his back arched in a curve.

Jago had used up vast quantities of energy but he would never quit now, for he was thoroughbred. Suddenly he found his second wind and flung himself forward even more violently.

The man sat tight, swaying with the horse's movements, but the sadistic smile had been wiped from his face. As the horse's anger turned to rage this communicated itself to him and he was having to work hard now to stay in the saddle. There was no time to spare to use the spurs. Would this horse never quit?

Jago reared high, standing almost vertical, swaying on his hocks to keep his balance. He felt the man's weight come right forward as balance was adjusted, and quick as a flash Jago plunged forward and stood on his front legs in an enormous kick. Both feet rose straight up in the air, then he became almost vertical the other way up, as he threw himself back on his hind legs.

Warrigan nearly went then. Such an extreme move, so cunningly tried, nearly foxed him. Frantically he reversed his balance, from leaning right forward to sitting right back, his black hair touching the red quarters. His face was crinkled now

with effort, and sweat poured down his cheeks in streams; his
jaws were set rigidly and he had drawn his tongue back to
safety. It would be easy to bite his own tongue in two. Even the
great Warrigan could now feel the tearing of tiring muscles,
even his own great thighs could only stand so much strain.
Surely the horse had to come down soon? He couldn't stay
vertical for ever—or could he? What was this creature, horse or
wild devil?

At last Jago dropped down to the ground again and with
tremendous cunning shot right up in another appallingly high
rear. His fighting strategy had changed now, his intelligent
brain was in command. Straightforward bucks and kicks were
wasted energy. Use the uncommon moves, catch the rider
unawares. He has hurt you, you hurt him! This hammered in
his brain, pain overrunning all else he had ever known from
man. Blood, fear, fright, and humiliation were all swept aside
by blinding, primeval rage.

Jago felt the tiniest give from his rider's knees and he swung
down again, shooting upwards in another enormous kick. His
head was ducked neatly between his forelegs, his back, quarters,
and hindlegs running in a straight line right into the bright blue
sky. He held this for three seconds, controlling his body with
marvellous balance, then he levelled himself and shot forward
in six large bucks.

Warrigan now knew fear. He had never ridden anything like
this before, this horse was mad, he was having a fit! He had
felt panic as his knee-grip loosened. Another two seconds and
he would have been off. Readjusting his broken balance he sat
upright again, riding the straightforward but easy bucks, his
head starting to snap from side to side as blood began trickling
down his left nostril from a broken capillary.

By all the gods, how much longer would this last?

Jago flung himself round at the rails, stretched with curving neck, opened his mouth, and with flattened ears tried to savage the rider's left knee. His teeth touched on each side of the patella, then the man's foot came back, and his heavy boot smashed into his mouth. At the same time the spurs slashed into his flanks again, this time digging to hurt and tear the flesh, cutting to draw blood. The bit sawed his head back straight, tearing through his mouth corners, opening bloody patches. At this moment Jago did go a little mad, the pain in his mouth was so excruciating.

Blinded with this pain, his plunges were but straightforward bucks and kicks, exhausting to perform but easier for the rider, and as Jago's brain took command again, he felt his rider firmly stuck in the saddle again. Sweating, bleeding, tired, he was just as determined not to quit.

The battle had been going on now for fifteen long minutes, watched by a silent crowd of white and black faces staring from around the railed paddock. It was obvious to all concerned that this was no ordinary breaking to saddle and rider. This battle was a blood-lust which could only end with one being hurt or perhaps even killed. But such a fight, once started, is quite impossible to stop.

To these onlookers it was incredible that two living beings could fight so long and so hard. What would be the horrible outcome? How did man and horse find the strength to keep going?

If they had thought a little, this would have been obvious. Jago was a thoroughbred who, once aroused, would die rather than quit, as indeed many a gallant horse has done in the past. Coupled with this fact was Jago's own make-up, his unusual breeding, the blood which had made him a rebel, and his hatred for being ridden. Another horse, even a thoroughbred, would probably have slowed down now or at least, paused to take breath before continuing the fight instead of just flailing on and on in wild rage.

It was the same with the man. Warrigan had never before been beaten by a horse. He was the champion rider for his race in that part of Australia and he was immensely proud of the fact that he could do something better than a white man—even his adored white boss. As well as this, Warrigan was undisputed cock of the walk on the station, lording it over all other members of his race, and he was perfectly aware that his loss of face would be terrible if he quit now. He would never live it down, life would become unbearable; he even had the shrewd suspicion that his gin would jeer at him, although he might beat her. He could not, he dare not, quit.

And so it was a stalemate. Each would continue fighting until both collapsed with utter exhaustion, and when they recovered they would get up and start all over again. There could be only one final outcome—a killing.

Mike Colston who had been on the scene the last few minutes took all this in, reached a sudden decision, and grabbed a rope.

"You and you, get over there! When I give the word, get Warrigan off!" he shouted, pointing to two of his mounted aborigines.

They cantered their horses to the gate and sat tensely waiting and watching their boss. Mike Colston climbed on to the fence and started spinning the rope in a loop over his head. Judging carefully he let the rope go. It flew through the air and landed neatly around the red colt's neck.

And so it was a stalemate

"Hold this rope, get in there!" shouted the stockman. "Get Warrigan off, that's an order!"

Jago was enraged when the rope again clutched at his windpipe. It was unfair, he had been doing fine and now other horses and men were intervening. He still had sense enough not to fight the rope. Opening his jaws he made another swinging grab to savage his rider's leg, but he was too late.

The mounted stockmen rode their horses up, crowding Jago against the rails. They lifted off the exhausted Warrigan and double-banked him out of the paddock back into the yard while Mike Colston kept the red colt tied to the stake.

Warrigan slid from the saddle, his feet touched the ground, and his knees crumpled. He fell heavily, sweat covering his body, his face plastered with blood, every muscle and bone shrieking in agony.

Mike Colston knelt worriedly and examined the best man he had.

"Get him into the bunkhouse!" he snapped as the man's eyes opened and stared up at him.

"Boss, boss! Leave the colt, don't—don't—!"

Mike Colston looked down at Warrigan and rested a hand on the still-shaking shoulder.

"He's only fit for shooting!"

"No, boss! Let him be, tomorrow I'll try again, I must—" pleaded the black man, feeling a moisture come into his eyes like a soft gin, a weak female.

Mike Colston stared back uneasily. He knew what was in Warrigan's head, he knew the sudden dread of losing face, the lowering of his status, his pride. The man was obsessed with beating the colt. He hesitated. He wanted no-one killed on his property, certainly not for the sake of a horse.

No wonder, he thought, I got him so dirt cheap. With trembling hands he rolled a cigarette, aware that the black eyes had never left his face.

"Boss?" pleaded Warrigan.

"O.K., old fella. But you're never to ride him without someone around. Take him in and see to him!"

Mike Colston turned, walked back to the rails, and looked at the still-straining colt. You wild devil, he thought, you near killed my best hand and you wouldn't have quit either. What the blazes made me buy you?

Jago stared back at the man, still a man but one with a different scent, and most important of all, not the man who had ridden him. He was wet all over from sweat, blood streamed down his flanks and dripped on to the ground, but his spirit was high. He had not thrown the man but nor had he ever stopped fighting him. If the other horses and men had not intervened he would have won, he knew.

"What about the horse, boss?"

The stockman turned to another of his men. "Leave him as he is with saddle and bridle on but cut the rope!"

"He might get down and bust the saddle!"

"Cheaper than busting someone's head!"

And so Mike Colston made another mistake. It was stupid and even cruel too to cut the rope but still leave the red colt bridled and saddled. The stockman was not a cruel man, he was harsh, but not vindictive. Perhaps he was afraid of someone being injured if he sent them to unsaddle the red colt, but he himself could have made the first attempt.

It is most probable that Jago would have stood quietly. He disliked saddles so much that it was a joy to have one removed from his back, and anyhow, although he fought, it was only

against a rider on his back or something which gave him direct
pain, like a rope.

So Jago was left standing all that evening and into the night
with the saddle on his back and the bridle on his head. He was
a bitterly confused horse by the time the dawn came; he was
also in considerable pain. The cuts on his flanks had dried and
scabs were already hardening on them; apart from the sharp
pain, little harm would come to him from them. He was too
young, too healthy, and had too strong a constitution. His
mouth was exquisite agony though. Both right and left mouth
corners were raw where the bit had rubbed and chafed the
flesh away in large running sores. These did not dry into protective scabs because of the saliva caused by the bit being left
in his mouth.

His confusion arose mostly from the fact that he was hungry.
He had burned up a considerable amount of energy in the fight
and now he wanted to eat. Always before, men had come with
food when he was hungry. This was something that had
happened since he was weaned from his dam. This logical
thing he had accepted as one of men's many laws. When a
horse was hungry then man gave him food—or alternatively,
he was turned into a pasture where he could help himself to
the grass. But this time man had done neither of these things;
never before in his whole life had Jago known such agony from
hunger. He was completely bewildered by this.

Unlike man, a horse likes to eat little and often. Nature
intended him to eat his way leisurely across ranges and prairies,
nibbling contentedly at will. No horse can function on an
empty stomach, least of all a domesticated, pampered thoroughbred who all his life has been waited on and provided for by
man.

Jago was losing faith rapidly. Apart from the hunger there was the saddle and bridle. After use, man always removed these, allowing the colt to stretch and roll and be free and easy. Here again, man was failing him. The saddle had not been removed, nor had the bridle; he was hungry and had not been fed. Jago's little, narrow world was crumbling before his very eyes and naturally he could not understand why. No one could explain to him, nor had he the reason to deduce the answer, so he stood sullenly, bitter resentment rising, faith and trust vanishing. Worst of all, savage hatred of man had been born in him.

He was not a horse whose spirit would ever be broken by pain and this harsh, totally unnecessary treatment, was turning him into a sullen, hating creature; and the fault belonged solely to man.

With the rising of the burning sun, a savage animal stood in the paddock, an animal totally different in temperament from the easy-going, good-natured racehorse, an animal consumed with the great fire of man-hate.

Jago had managed to drink from the water trough in the night and indeed the tepid water had eased some of the first fierce pain in his mouth but it was hunger which now demanded all his attention.

There was not a blade of grass in the paddock, not a leaf or a twig. The earth was dry, hard-packed, and naked. Jago had even gnawed at the rails, trying to find something to quell the griping pains in his rumbling stomach, but having been pampered all his life he spat out the coarse bark from the timber poles.

He had not attempted to remove the saddle in the night. His flanks were too sore to allow him to get down and roll but he had rubbed against the rails, hopefully trying to remove the saddle's weight. The girth was still tight, and he had slight cramps around his middle and a wild desire to indulge in the ecstasy of a free stretch, but this was denied while the saddle was there. He had gingerly rubbed his head along the gate, hoping this would remove the bridle at least, but the throatlash had been fastened too securely. In a sudden fit of spite he had attacked the trailing reins, rearing and stamping on them, venting his fiery temper until he had only hurt himself the more by treading on the reins and lifting his head at the same time, so tearing his sore mouth afresh.

It was a sullen animal which confronted Mike Colston the next morning, a wild, bitter animal whose mood was only too plain for all to see.

Warrigan limped from the bunkhouse where he had spent the night and, leaning against the gate, watched the colt.

"That's one bad horse, boss!"

"Too right, Warrigan. He's standing there with enough poison in him to kill us all," grunted Mike Colston.

"I try again, later when the sun goes down," said the black man, his pride bitterly hurt.

"You'll do no such thing! What chance do you think you have of staying on him with all those pulled muscles! He'd have you off in a flash and you'd be pounded flatter than a witchetty grub underfoot. No, I'll have a shot. Let him stand a bit longer with an empty belly. See if that takes some of the fight out of him."

"But, boss, I'm the horse-breaker here and—"

"And I'm the boss, Warrigan! You can try another day when those muscles are back in shape. You go off back to that gin of yours. She'll be wondering what's happened!" said the stockman, putting an affectionate hand on Warrigan's shoulder, looking him straight in the eyes.

The black man looked back. He knew his boss understood his pride and he also knew that the boss would not stick on the red colt, empty belly or not. That horse had too much fight and murder in his heart to be put off by something like an empty stomach. He was the type of horse that would still be fighting when down on the ground dying. He was that rarest of animals, the horse who would never quit—and Warrigan wanted to have the pleasure of mastering him. He *had* to have that pleasure to keep face. Let the boss have a go, he'd get nowhere, and when he, the great Warrigan, was fit again, let the devil in the red colt watch out!

CHAPTER FOUR

Victory!

AND so Michael Colston, stockman, made the greatest mistake of all. He underestimated the red colt's abilities, he thought that with hunger and pain some of the fight and strength would be licked out of the colt. He did not understand that these very things were making him more bad-tempered and vicious with every hour that went by. If some great rider had ridden the horse to a standstill and then bossed him into obedience, he might conceivably have made him amenable and suitable for use. But Mike Colston was certainly not that man, good rider though he was.

To give Mike Colston his due, he was man enough and leader enough not to expect someone else to do what he couldn't do himself. To keep *his* own face and respect it was necessary to try and ride the colt. He did not like the idea, he did not even fancy walking into the paddock and going near the red colt, but it had to be done and because he feared what might happen the stockman sent his wife and children out on a picnic, neither telling them his plan nor fooling his shrewd wife in the very least. Wise and understanding woman though, she understood even if she did not agree. In the outback of the great heart of Australia a man must be a man or go under.

As the sun started sliding down the sky Mike Colston grabbed a rope, caught the colt, and fastened him to the rails again. He stood awhile just watching the horse, noting his expression, observing his mood, and sorting out his own emotions. He was sweating across the forehead but whether it was from the heat of the day or from fear he didn't quite know.

He hoped it was not the sweat of fear because nothing is so discernible to any animal as man's fright. And an obviously clever, intelligent animal like the red colt would soon turn that fright to his own advantage.

Jago stared back at the white man, a different man from the one who rode him yesterday but nevertheless—a man! Man, the giver of pain, the giver of hunger, the betrayer of faith. Man—the enemy!

Jago's hunger was by now so intense that pain from his mouth and flanks had been pushed aside. His stomach emitted rumble after groaning rumble as it protested for food, and he could think of nothing else. Memories of the good grass and feeds he had been used to in Victoria were still acutely fresh.

Now that the rope was around his neck, however, the hunger urge began to give way to anger. Yesterday's hurt and misery were still vividly present in his brain and the red ears went back as the white man climbed over the rails.

Jago watched as he started a slow walk towards him, then all the pain, hunger, and misery rose like a rocket. He rolled his eyes, opened his mouth, and screeched. Then he charged at the man, murder in his heart, revenge screaming from every muscle and nerve.

The man took one look at the horse's expression, the open mouth, the large teeth, and in one swift movement reversed on his tracks and vaulted back over the rails. Jago slithered to a halt and reared in frustration, snapping at the air, striking at the rails with his feet, forgetting the rope as he plunged to right and left.

He jolted back in his tracks as he overstepped the rope's

length. Still in a rage, he turned and attacked, striking at the rope with feet and teeth, making up for the frustration of losing the man. But he had not yet learned that to cut a rope it must be taut. His efforts wasted energy, re-opened his wounds, and were quite futile.

He was so absorbed in what he was doing that he forgot to watch the man and when the second rope snaked around his neck he stopped in surprise. This rope was made fast so that the red colt was held from both sides close to the rails.

By the time Jago decided to attack again it was too late. He could move neither backwards nor forwards, left nor right.

Mike Colston had now been joined by two other men who controlled the ropes, keeping them taut.

"Don't loose those ropes until I give the word!" ordered the stockman as he clambered on the fence again.

Jago rolled his eyes at the man, snapped with his jaws, missed, and his nose was seized tightly. He struggled, straining to breathe, not having the sense to anticipate this move and hold his breath as a man would. He grunted and squirmed while the man gingerly clambered on to the ground, keeping a wary eye on the stamping legs. Jago could see what was going to happen but was quite powerless to do anything. Just as he found he could breathe again he felt the man's weight lurch into the saddle again.

He began to whip around, remembered the ropes in time, and stood shuddering with impatience to start the fight, pain and hunger now completely forgotten.

"Oke! Get those ropes off but hang around!"

The stock-hands loosened the ropes, expertly tossing them off the colt's neck with a wrist-flip, and Jago shot round in his tracks, bucking hard within seconds. Each buck now had just that fraction more venom because of the other day's pain.

Jago could feel that this new rider was equally firm so without wasting further time on bucking he put into practice some of the tactics which he now knew would loosen a rider's seat.

He shot straight up in a rear, balancing himself beautifully, then shooting down reversed himself in a double kick, head between his forelegs. He unloosened himself with a fly-jump then spun round in his tracks, propping sharply to either side, leaning so far that it seemed he must topple over.

Jago felt his rider's knees sliding on the saddle flaps, there was a loose bumping in the saddle seat, and maliciously he continued twirling around in hard jolts, tail flailing, mane whipping.

Mike Colston had ridden many rough horses but this was the first time he had tried to sit one which thought and planned deadly moves like this. He knew his seat was loosening however much he might struggle and strain. The continual circular movement was making him dizzy. Soon he knew he would be off.

His right leg swayed away from the saddle, daylight showed beneath his thighs, and suddenly he was going. Releasing the reins, kicking his other leg free, he flung out an arm as he hurtled through the air. He landed heavily, rolling over and over with his own momentum, then head buzzing he climbed to his feet.

Jago careered on down the paddock in joy at having thrown the man, then turning saw him slowly climbing to his feet. There he was, man the enemy! Without a thought he charged straight at the stockman, mouth open, ears back, hatred obvious.

The stockman stood a second, appalled at the ferocity in the horse's face, then forgetting his aches and spinning head, he staggered and ran for the safety of the fence. He flung himself over the rails and dropped down the far side just as Jago crashed against the fence, making it shudder in the ground.

Screeching and snapping, Jago raged at the man, then stamping his feet he flung himself around the paddock once more, kicking wildly, celebrating his victory. It was not so hard to throw a man after all, and when chased, man fled. Two valuable pieces of information were stored away in his brain, lessons which he would never forget.

Mike Colston stood rubbing his head, muttering angrily to himself as Warrigan limped up to join him.

"He's a devil!" snorted the stockman.

"A wild horse that one, but wait another day or so, I really ride him!"

"O.K., you have another go—but not with those spurs. That horse doesn't want any needling and I don't want him cut up any more!"

Warrigan scowled at this order but was wise enough not to question it. The touch of sadism in his nature had always been revealed by the way he used spurs and the stockman knew this. He had already decided that it had been a mistake to allow Warrigan to try the horse first wearing spurs. The damage was done now and the horse had to be ridden to a standstill, but further spurring would only make him worse.

"We'll leave him a couple of days, let him out into the larger paddock, but we must get that saddle and bridle off. Hey! Rope that colt from both sides so that he can be unsaddled!"

The two mounted stockmen, who had been interested spectators of their boss's futile attempt on the red colt, nodded, uncoiled the ropes, and caught the still bucking and kicking Jago.

Jago saw the ropes coming, tried to dodge them, and failed. They plopped round his neck and he swerved to a halt, anxious not to hurt himself by struggling but equally determined that no-one else was going to get on his back.

The ropes were fastened tightly and Mike Colston approached with a scarf in his hand. He kept it out of sight while he climbed the rails, dodging the red colt's snapping teeth, then in a second he covered the blazing eyes.

Jago froze as sight vanished, and again he started trembling. Of all the man-horrors this blindness was the worst. He could feel himself wanting to explode in every direction but he dare not move without sight. He flinched as hands unfastened the girth and one ear came forward at this interesting move. They were taking off the saddle! He stood, anxious to be free of the leather and made not the slightest attempt to bite as the bit and bridle were removed.

The stockman climbed back on top of the rails, whipped away the blindfold and quickly dropped down to safety against Warrigan. The ropes were loosened and shaken off and Jago shot aside. He was free again. The bliss of having no girth around his middle, the utter joy of being able to roll and stretch!

He lay and rolled vigorously in the dust, stretching and pushing his muscles, snorting to himself, his temper improving with every movement. Satisfied at last, he scrambled to his feet, walked over to the trough and drank. Slowly he sucked the water down his throat, relishing the freedom as he drank, and when he had finished he lifted his head and stared pointedly at the stockman, water dribbling from his lips.

"All right, turn him into the bottom paddock, there's feed there!"

The hands opened the bottom gate, tucking themselves behind the timber for safety's sake.

Jago watched the gate open and with curiosity and caution mingling he walked quietly down and stood half-way in and half-way out, looking around him.

Making up his mind he pushed forward into a springy trot then bounced into a canter. Here was grass, here was food, and he was so very hungry.

But Jago had a shock. This coarse grass was not what he had been used to. Always fed the very best since a foal, he was appalled and disappointed at the poor fare before him; but a horse or man will eat almost anything if really hungry, so he started to graze.

He snapped impatiently at the grown, thready grass, pulling some out by the roots in his eagerness to appease his hunger. With the important business of eating he forgot his enemy man and it was not until late in the night that he was sufficiently full to lift his head and just stand staring out over the bush from where such fascinating scents and sounds were coming.

They left him in the paddock for three days, giving his flanks time to heal and his mouth to acquire a protective scab. The fine mouth which he had developed from a careful breaking was quite ruined and would never be the same again. From now on it would harden and toughen until it lost all feeling and sensitivity. This was the direct result of the black stockman's ham-handed, rough attempt to outride him. The red colt had been completely ruined. Only a very understanding and patient rider would ever be able to re-educate Jago now and it is doubtful if the harsh, busy life of the outback had a man of that calibre.

Jago lost flesh rapidly, which was only to be expected, but as he learned how to live on the poorer grass his body started to adapt itself. He had never been a fat horse and the training as a racehorse had developed his muscles to a high degree.

These muscles were now to become even tougher, not from training but from Jago's new way of life. During those days in the paddock he learned another valuable lesson—how to search for food. The paddock was large, roaming down over the land in slopes and rises and enclosed by wire fencing; the feed was there, but patchy.

Always before, Jago had just put his head down and eaten his fill. Now he had to walk around, trying this and testing that, hunting and searching for the best grass. This kept him continuously occupied and, even when the sun blazed down with its midday heat, he was still eating.

At night he would stop and half doze, standing up. He would suddenly awake automatically and stand listening, highly alert, to the bush noises. There was so much that was unfamiliar and being intelligent he was eager and curious to learn.

Sometimes he felt lonely for the company of other horses because like all of his species he was a gregarious creature. He would lift his head and scream out a whinny, part question, part invitation. He would receive replies, curious and friendly, which made him trot restlessly around the paddock but there was no way of getting out. The wire fence was too high and the sharp barbs stopped him trying to rub a post down.

It was the first time he had met barbed wire and an inquiring nose poked on to the sharp point of a barb received a quick prick, making him jump back in shock. After that, he left the fence alone. He did not need a repeat lesson.

At the end of the three days he was back to his normal

health and strength. He had forgotten the wounds on his flanks
and mouth, he was full of food which he had found himself, he
had not been short of water, and the delightful freedom of
roaming at will had eased some of the restless feeling in his
body.

When the three horsemen rode into the paddock swinging
their ropes he shot away from them, angry at their intrusion. It
did not yet occur to him to attack them and drive them away;
a horse and rider were still too big a combination for him to
tackle and as yet there was no reason to challenge them.

Jago thrust himself into his fast, racing gallop which drew
gasps of admiration from Mike Colston, Warrigan, and another
aborigine stockman. How that colt could run!

They chased him down to the end of the paddock, pinning
him against the fence. At the realization that he was trapped,
Jago's temper started flaring. Wildly he half reared, trying to
find an escape, but the only way was forward. He could not
move any further backward without going on to the barbed
wire fence so he shot forward, his head low, trying to dodge
the ropes, and this time his ruse succeeded.

With his nostrils almost brushing the dust it was quite
impossible for a rope to be thrown around his neck and this
fact was instantly understood by Jago as he galloped glee-
fully up the paddock again with the slower stockhorses in
pursuit.

For fifteen minutes he led the men a merry dance. Each time
they trapped him at a fence he spun and charged back at them,
dodging, swerving, and always with lowered head evading the
ropes.

Cunning as Jago's moves were, however, the men's minds
were superior and gradually they forced him into a tight little

corner, riding their horses in a sideways passage so that no gap was left through which he could dart.

Now Jago began to be frightened. He was completely trapped, and panic-stricken, he flung himself to right and left, seeking a loophole, hunting for the tiniest passageway to escape. Finding none, he automatically backed away from the approaching men whose object was to pin him against the fence with their horses' bodies while they roped him.

Jago forgot the fence and backed too far, the sharp barbs digging into his quarters. He shot forward like a scalded cat and without really thinking about the move he hurtled towards Warrigan's horse. The two animals crashed together, the ridden horse screeching in shock and objection, but Jago was in terror now. His way was still partially blocked so opening his mouth he bit the ridden horse angrily.

The horse squealed in pain and anger and, ignoring his rider, danced quickly away from the red savage, and Jago shot through to freedom again. The men swung around after him, cursing wildly, knowing that in a flat-out gallop they had no hope of catching the red colt.

Mike Colston saw Jago was running free and easily, with his head extended, and standing in the stirrups he decided to try a long shot with the rope. It seemed a waste of effort, an improbable shot, but by one of those rare chances it succeeded. The rope sped out, dancing through the heat haze, straight as an arrow, and plopped squarely around Jago's neck.

The stockman swiftly wound the end of the rope around his saddle and backed his trained horse who took the strain.

"Get some more ropes on him, quickly, in case he charges me!" roared the stockman as he started playing the irate horse on his straining rope.

Jago knew the futility of pulling against the rope so he decided to try a tactic which had already worked once. He flung himself into a gallop and charged wildly at Mike Colston.

He looked a ferocious beast as he hurtled nearer, his feet lashing the ground and raising clouds of dust, his eyes red with rage, his ears back flat against his poll, and his mouth wide open, showing large and ugly teeth.

But this time the charge was his undoing. It allowed the other two men to take careful aim and two more ropes dropped around the red colt's neck, pulling him to a braking standstill as the strain was taken at right angles.

And so Jago learned something else: that a man with a rope, whether on foot or mounted, is one of the greatest threats to freedom. Beware all men with ropes, warned his brain, and this priceless piece of information was stored away never to be forgotten.

Jago hung his head in sullen anger as he was led away. He longed to strike at the men and their horses but they were keeping a discreet distance, well out of range of teeth or heels.

At this point, he was as dangerous as he had ever been because he knew for a fact that man was not invincible. He had also overcome that fear of man inherent in most hoofed animals, and instead of running away he knew now to turn and attack. The lion, tiger, and wolf have always known this but only a few horses ever understand it. Mostly they turn and flee, relying upon their superior speed, but the red colt had learned the vice of attacking, the strange, exhilarating joy of throwing himself forward, ready with teeth and heels. With this new and not unpleasant battle lust, he had discovered just how puny man is when face to face with a horse.

They took him back into the smaller paddock, tied him

firmly, put on the blindfold, and when he was standing quietly threw the heavy saddle on his back and forced the bridle on his head.

"Sure you're O.K., Warrigan?" asked Mike Colston a little anxiously.

"Sure boss, I'm O.K!" replied the aborigine who felt naked without his spurs. In fact he was not at all sure. He, too, was experiencing strange, new emotions. For the first time in his life, the great Warrigan of Bereeba station was badly afraid. He did not show his fright but it was there inside his heart.

The instant the man climbed on to his back, Jago felt two things: the way this man sat and gripped meant it was the one who had hurt him so much before; also, the rider was now afraid. The man's fear-scent made Jago flare his nostrils pleasurably.

Mike Colston, who knew a horse and its moods, was watching closely and frowned uneasily.

"Let 'im go!" shouted Warrigan.

The ropes loosened, Jago whipped around, and the fight was on again.

"Get a rifle from the house, quick boy, now!" snapped the stockman to his son who was watching with excited eyes. Shaken by the tone in his father's voice, the boy flew to obey.

As Jago bolted down the paddock, plunging and rocking, only one thought dominated his mind; on his back was the man who had given him so much fear and pain, his sore flanks, his bloody mouth—they had all come from this rider—and now he was gripped with the sweat of fear.

He reversed at the paddock end and started working through his repertoire. Bucks changed to propping swerves which ended with kicks, and in the exact middle of the dry ground he started his rearing and kicking, body vertical, see-sawing its direction in rapid momentum.

Warrigan gripped furiously, his fear being replaced with some anger and his determination to stay on the red colt crystallizing with every movement the horse made. Now that he was actually riding, he had not time to be really afraid. He swung backwards and forwards, timing his moves to the rears and kicks, first leaning forward so that his face brushed the red mane, then swinging himself back so that his hair brushed the colt's quarters. His timing was precise and superb, the judgment acquired from years spent riding wild brumbies to a stand-still.

Watching intently, Mike Colston let out his breath slowly in admiration for Warrigan's polished horsemanship, at the same time carefully cradling the rifle in his arms.

Jago suddenly realized that he was getting nowhere; he also deduced that the rider was no longer afraid. His grip was, if anything, even more rigid, and the fear-scent had vanished giving way to the anger-scent.

The colt changed his tactics again and started bucking on one spot, flinging himself around in a tight little circle, using the movements which had unseated the stockman.

Warrigan sat up firmly, leaning just a little backward. He kept his eyes wide open, staring straight ahead, marvelling at the rapidly changing scenery until the dust rose to such a height that it clung around his face. His body was whipping like a new lash but he knew he was as firm and strong as the great sun herself. He suddenly knew he could outride this horse, he would be master yet.

Jago was frustrated. The man was still there! He spun down

the paddock, trying a short burst of bucking, and a niggle of doubt started pounding in his heart. This man wasn't going to move; he would be ridden to a standstill.

Then his cunning, intelligent brain took over. There was still one move he had not tried. Without hesitation, Jago hurtled around and galloped straight down the paddock, not bucking or kicking but running dead flat and smooth.

Six paces from the rails Jago hurled himself into the air, his red body apparently flying onward, then without hesitation he deliberately threw himself sideways to the ground.

Man and horse hit the hard earth with a fearful crash and for three seconds were invisible in the dust. Mike Colston yelled and lifting the rifle ran frantically down the rails.

Jago was winded and he lay still, snorting to draw his breath, and under him the rider screamed in agony where his broken leg was being splintered and crushed even more by the colt's weight. Catching his breath, Jago flung out his forelegs and strained to stand.

Warrigan screamed once more then his head rolled sideways and he fell silent. Mike Colston vaulted the rails and charged towards the dust cloud, his rifle at the ready. Eight yards away, other men ran to assist.

Jago stood, slightly shocked and bemused, then his brain cleared and he understood his victory. He snorted, scrambled round, looked down at the man and half reared, screaming rage, defiance, and revenge.

Here was the enemy, the giver of pain, and he screamed again as he rose, high forelegs dangling, ready to drop and pound the man to pieces. He had the shock of his life when the stockman burst through the cloud, grasped the situation in a flash, reversed the rifle, and slammed the heavy stock on Jago's nose.

The man's appearance was so sudden and unexpected that Jago lost his balance. He strained with his hocks, scrabbled with his feet, then it was too late. He overbalanced backwards and crashed down for the second time.

"Get Warrigan out of here—but go easy, watch that leg!" roared the stockman while, legs apart, straddling the earth, he glared at the red colt.

Jago scrambled to his feet and stood shaking. For a second he did not know what to do. His head hurt but he was more shocked than anything else. He had never before even considered such a blow. As he stood, however, his temper began churning again. So all men truly were enemies. No matter what their colour or scent, they all gave pain, they all broke trust. All that stood facing him now was one man alone. Just one man between himself and the rider. And Jago had already learned that when he charged, a man on foot ran.

He reared high, screaming his challenge, and charged at the stockman.

Mike Colston slung the rifle to his shoulder and with only the briefest of sighting pulled the trigger. The rifle boomed loudly in his ear and he aimed for another shot.

Again Jago had a shock. He had never heard a gun fire before and he was astonished when the bullet ploughed a furrow of fire along his shoulders. He braked, swerving sideways, his challenge collapsing like a damp firework. He wanted to jump at the gun's boom and leap aside from the pain in his shoulder but he did neither, he just stared at the man.

He saw the rifle clunk back against the man's shoulder, his quick eyes noticed the movement of a finger, and his intelligent brain screamed a warning. He spun around and fled to the end of the paddock, making no attempt to come down and fight while the stockman stood there with the rifle.

And so Jago learned another priceless lesson: that a man on foot with a gun must be absolutely feared. The long sticklike thing that spoke with such noise, that spat such pain from a distance, was the most terrible, the most ultimate of weapons. With the gun, man was again the supreme being and a horse must bow down and give way to him.

For the rest of his life Jago was to remember with appalling clarity the first time he saw a gun fired, and never again did he ever make the futile attempt to challenge an armed man.

Nature never gives an animal the chance to learn a lesson twice. He either takes advantage of the first lesson or pays the price of stupidity and Jago was anything but stupid.

He was angry still, and ready and willing to continue a fight with any rider, but he had no intention of walking down the paddock until the stockman and his assistants had carried the silent Warrigan away out of sight. And it was a full hour before he walked slowly down, lowered his head, and gingerly sniffed at the hated scent. It was only then that the temper rose again and he danced around in the dust, pounding the scent into oblivion, until satisfied at last, he walked over to the trough and drank his fill.

He waited quietly for the men to come with the ropes to remove the saddle, which they did in time, and this he suffered without remonstrance.

If Peter Huston had walked into the paddock he would not have recognized his red colt; the anger and hate poured from the clever eyes like searchlights. And the intelligent head was never still for one second. Already, like any wild animal, Jago was alert for danger. His vigilance never lapsed, day or night.

Only the domesticated, trusting animal relaxes his guard for sleep.

Jago's senses and nerves were as sharply tuned as those of the brumby horse born wild in the outback. His retrogression was practically complete.

CHAPTER FIVE

The Buckjumper

THE next day Mike Colston stood with his wife Betty, leaning on the paddock rails, morosely eyeing the red colt.

Jago watched them from a distance of four yards, listening to the negative tone of their voices as they talked. He realized that no harm could come to him at this moment; the man was the other side of the fence and no ropes or guns were visible.

"And what now?" asked Betty Colston. "Warrigan will be lucky if he ever rides again. He has a terrible fracture, he certainly won't be able to ride rough horses again."

"No. I regret the day I ever saw that horse! And I blame myself for Warrigan. I should have supervised him when he rode the colt. He *is* rough, especially with those confounded spurs of his. I think none of this would have arisen if the colt had been handled more quietly from the start, but it's too late now. That colt is full of hate."

"What are you going to do with him?"

"I could shoot him and cut my loss," and Mike Colston gave a feeble laugh. "That's just what I told his breeder, too. No, I think I'll turn him out with the other colts for a spell, fatten him up a bit, heal those wounds, then I'll sell him as a buckjumper."

"Of course! He'll be perfect for the rodeos."

"And I don't care where he goes as long as he leaves here.

That animal is a menace. You've told the children not to attempt to go near him?"

"Yes, they won't touch him. They're as frightened of him as I am."

"Well, it's cured me of wanting a racer. I'll stick to the stock-horses."

Later on, mounted riders turned the colt into the large paddock and opening the bottom gate drove him out into the large pasture where ran a number of the station horses—two-year olds, three-year olds and a few yearlings.

Jago bounced through the gate then braked to an abrupt halt, staring at the interested horses. He flared his nostrils, taking in the various scents, and with stiff legs and exaggerated steps walked forward.

Heads were lifted high, lips touched, squeals challenged, tails flickered, as they clustered around him. A few hind legs were flicked in warning, two horses reared in challenge, and Jago laid his ears back.

Here was the companionship which he had so desired but here he would have to make his mark. With most animals, there is an order of precedence—a leader with his lieutenant and then the rest falling away in status to the most humble member who is bullied by everyone, rather like the "pecking" order of hens.

Jago had never met with this order of rank and prerogative before but he accepted it automatically and promptly established his own place in the line of respect.

He screeched a warning, kicked, and reared high, challenging the leader. Without hesitation the challenge was accepted. In great interest the rest of the horses backed in a half circle.

Jago had never fought another horse in his life but fighting was a natural thing to him. Since his arrival on the station he had learned the fact that he who attacks first, without delay, is often the winner.

As dogs go through certain preliminaries before fighting, so do horses. The dog's hackles will rise while he announces his intention to fight; this is then accompanied by a strutting, stiff-legged gait, and finally the attack.

Horses also make these battle announcements before actually fighting. They bounce up and down with half rears, squeal their intentions for all to hear, lay their ears back, and sometimes snake their necks low over the ground; only then can they fight.

But not so with Jago. He had learned that the first in action is the winner. He wasted no time in going through the pre-fight routine. While the leader started his dance of challenge, Jago charged without pause or hesitation.

His red body cannoned into the leader's brown one and in a second he had toppled him over ignominiously on to the ground. Jago whipped round, the battle lust flaring, and as the brown horse struggled to his feet, Jago's body thudded into him again. For the second time the brown horse rolled in an ungainly heap in the dust.

Jago spun on his hocks, half rearing in his haste to carry the fight even further into the enemy's camp, and hurtled down at the brown horse again. He was fantastically quick in every move and the brown horse thrashed wildly to regain his feet in time. Quite off balance, his enemy half reared as Jago crashed on to him, striking with his forelegs rather like a boxer. The two heads snaked in and out, biting and chewing, then Jago swung round, dropped his head, and let fly a double-barrel kick, the blows landing with a rumble on the brown's ribs.

The brown horse grunted with pain and shock and decided the leadership wasn't worth all this. Turning, he galloped off out of sight. Jago chased him a few paces to drive the lesson home, then returned with bouncing steps snorting his challenge to any other contender. None came forward.

And so Jago established his leadership of the gang of horses. When he strode forward they all backed away. The path ahead, clear of obstacles, was his alone, and naturally the best feed belonged to him. After all, he had fought for the right and won.

For a number of weeks Jago lived a carefree, happy life. He was untroubled by men, he had his place as horse leader, there was feed in plenty, and out here in the great open he was able to indulge his curiosity, to watch and learn, to listen and identify.

The first time he saw a kangaroo he had stopped grazing, stared in astonishment, and followed curiously as the large buck kangaroo bounded slowly ahead followed by his wives. Their scents were fascinating to Jago, their peculiar action astonishing, and it was only when the large kangaroo halted to challenge Jago's closing proximity, that he stopped and backed away. His instincts told him he was trespassing. There were young in their mothers' pouches and he gave ground without question because that was the law handed down to him from his ancestors. When the females had young, then the leaders must protect them from all comers. Jago never thought to challenge or fight; the large kangaroo was only following the natural law and it was he who was in the wrong.

Rabbits he knew and therefore ignored, but snakes were a different matter. He had not met a snake before, which was his good fortune because snakes are common all over Australia. The first time he saw a snake basking in the sun he stared in wonder, at the same time aware of the crinkling under his skin, the odd feeling which he knew was alarm. He did not have to be told that here was an enemy, he just knew it was so.

The snake moved lazily, annoyed at being disturbed; opening its jaws, the tongue flashed in and out while the large fangs were ready to drop into position for a strike. The poison sacs were full, their dose highly lethal, and Jago went no nearer. His valuable inherited instinct told him to let well alone. He often saw other snakes and once a large one, quite as long as a tall man with a body as thick as his own forearm. Again he left this snake alone though he would have been quite safe sniffing at it because it happened to be a large carpet snake; non-venomous, it kills by constriction only.

One of the most peculiar animals Jago met was a great goanna or frilled lizard. He saw this creature walking slowly over the ground in a rippling movement and he went to investigate. The lizard halted and turned to face him, then before Jago's startled eyes a large frill rose, ten inches across, and the lizard stood on its hind legs. The jaws opened showing a mouth of fierce teeth, the skin, brown on top with a yellow-green underside, was hard and spiky, and the whole appearance was so utterly ferocious that Jago hastily backed away from the creature's path and made no attempt to interfere.

He often saw these lizards and gradually learned that they were quite harmless to him, their frightening appearance being their defence.

He often found the odd bandicoot and once, in sheer mischief, chased one of these lop-eared creatures to its burrow. He knew the opossums well and had often stood at night, watching them wake up and come out to feed and play in the trees, their black tails dangling carelessly from the branches.

One never-to-be-forgotten day he met another queer and unknown animal. The porcupine ant eater had just fed well on a large nest of ants and was feeling lazy and satisfied with the world, far to idle to move away when the curious colt approached.

Jago lowered his head to sniff at this strange creature, then extended his lips to investigate. The sharp quills rose, pricking his lips badly. Jago forgot his dignity and bolted in shock and pain. Never again did he make the same mistake.

It was only by trial and error that he found out about the other denizens of the bush. If he had been a foal, his dam would have watched over him and taught him what was safe and what was dangerous. Jago could only teach himself, and compared to the other horses, he was still very inexperienced. The only thing in which he over-rode them was his skill, strength, speed, and temper when it came to fighting. In this, he was quite supreme.

He did not have to be taught to fight, he already knew it as the young lion or tiger cub does, and coupled with this knowledge was his fantastic speed. All horses are quick, for this is part of nature's defence for them, but Jago was in a class of his own. Perhaps it was his superior brain or the fact that from a foal he had always eaten the best of foods, but his reflexes were conditioned to such a pitch that at times his lightning movements were difficult to follow with the eye.

He had learned from his battles with the riders that ferocity is a fighter's greatest asset when combined with courage never to quit. He had learned too that immediate attacks with no preliminaries led to sudden surprise, this had been confirmed when he had so easily beaten the brown horse in disputing the right to be leader.

Those weeks spent running loose and away from man were another valuable part of his education which were to stand him in good stead later on in his life.

It was with a distinct shock one morning that Jago saw the riders coming slowly towards the group of horses.

He trotted to the front, staring long and hard, deciding whether he should fight or flee. He had no jot of fear for the men now and only contempt for their horses but he had to make sure exactly what weapons the men carried.

Jago knew instinctively that they were coming for him.

He saw the coiled ropes in the riders' right hands, he saw too the long rifle under the stockman's arm and without waiting for further confirmation he turned and fled for his freedom.

The men let out a yell and chased after him, scattering through the group of puzzled and excited horses.

Jago bolted into his superb racing gallop, his legs tearing over the hard ground, skidding down the slopes, scrambling up the hills, but never pausing to draw breath or look behind. He galloped wildly forward, head high, ears back, eyes rolling in anger.

He had no need to turn and look at his pursuers; a horse has protruding eyes and with these and his ears he can easily estimate danger in his rear. Jago knew he was drawing well away from the riders but he did not decrease his speed. The sight of the ropes had made him realize that his freedom was threatened and when he had been caught before it had always been for the saddle and rider.

He careered across the open bushland until in the far distance he saw the twinkles as the sun shone on wire fencing. Without pausing, he swung aside and darted in another direction. A fallen gum tree lay in his path—he pressed with his hocks and

jumped it with feet to spare. Then there was a dry river bed—
he crashed over the hard stony ground, clattered up the far
side, wove through a cluster of yellow wattle trees, and shot
ahead. He knew he had outdistanced the riders for the hoof-
beats sounded far away now. What he did not know was that
the quick-thinking men had formed two parties. As Jago
stormed ahead in his wild gallop, a silent group of riders
was waiting directly in his path, half hidden behind some
shrubs.

Jago saw them but far too late. He braked to a halt, his feet
slithering, his body swaying with the abrupt stop, but before he
could turn at a tangent, the ropes were around his neck and the
riders were pulling on both sides.

Jago kicked in anger, trying to reach home and do damage,
but he knew from past experience he would be unlucky. He
had never thought to look ahead for his enemies, he had only
concentrated upon his rear. He would never make that mistake
again.

They led the infuriated horse back to the station yard,
keeping the ropes very tight and making sure that their horses
did not step too near either teeth or heels.

Jago was humiliated as well as furious. His capture in front
of the horses he had led was appalling. He knew that if he
regained his freedom now he would be expected to fight for
the leadership again, to prove himself once more. This realization made his mood more savage and he was a dangerous animal
as he stood in the yard, firmly tied but highly alert to the
slightest sign of inattention from the riders around him.

"How you going to get him in the truck, boss?" one man
asked, hoping that he would not be expected to lead the wild
red colt in.

Mike Colston handled his long stock-whip. "With this if necessary!"

But the stockman had used his head. A large feed was prepared where the red colt could see and smell it; this was taken slowly into the horse truck and placed in a feed bowl.

Slowly Jago's ears came forward as he caught the smell of oats—that delicious, mouth-watering food which he had not tasted for such a long time. Immediately, thinking back to the Victorian stud days, he stepped forward to follow the tantalizing food, but the ropes checked. Back came his ears again.

Mike Colston studied the colt's mood. He dare not risk loosening the ropes altogether just in case the horse took it into his head to attack. Would he follow the food with the ropes trailing loosely but held ready to be tightened again? Gingerly, he signalled to his men.

Jago felt the ropes loosening and was torn by two emotions: the desire to attack these men who had dragged him away from his freedom and the lure of the wonderful food. His stomach won over his heart and slowly he walked across the yard, up the ramp, and hastily put his head into the feed bowl, half afraid the oats might have vanished. He heard the clunk as the ramp thudded up behind but paid no attention. He was far too busy eating and anyhow he was an experienced traveller. He had never known pain or fear when enclosed in a truck and in fact his journeys had always been pleasant with the plentiful food men had given him to keep him quiet.

This truck was no exception. Apart from the oats there was hay and a small bowl, fixed into the truck's side, which held water. Quite contentedly he settled down, eating quickly, and he was not even aware of the ropes being cut as the doors were firmly fastened.

The engine grunted into life but Jago took not the slightest notice. The oats had gone and now he turned his attention to the hay. After the coarse feed in the paddock it was bliss to eat such marvellous food and all without the effort of hunting for it!

He travelled through the night and part of the next day but food was given to him regularly by the travelling attendant and it was an interested but calm horse who trotted from the truck into yet another small railed yard when the journey ended.

Jago's first impression was of noise, confusion, and many men. There seemed to be men everywhere. Crowded around the outside of the rails, two and in places three deep, they shouted amongst themselves as Jago walked around swishing his tail.

"He don't look very wild!"

"Five pound you go in there and saddle him!"

"That's a real beaut of a horse!"

"Look at that head! That's a blood horse, that is!"

The men's noises were a cacophony in Jago's head and he stared curiously as he walked around. There were other horses somewhere, he could hear them and smell them, and he blared forth a challenging whinny, anxious to establish himself as leader once more.

He ignored the men after a while; they were on the other side of the rails and impossible for him to reach with teeth or heels so he concentrated on trying to understand where he was. The man smell was everywhere, the scent so thick and heavy it was almost overpowering to his nostrils. But this was nothing to the noises—not just men noises but those from trucks and machines.

Jago was not to know that he was in the small horse pens at the Brisbane Exhibition Ground and that he would himself be taking part in the show as a buckjumper.

The Exhibition show, or the "Ekka", ran for a week as did the respective shows in the other state capitals and it was for this that Jago had again changed hands.

Good buckjumping horses were not easily found. Plenty of horses could and would buckjump but usually they became tired and desisted. Jago's reputation had enabled Mike Colston to recover some of his purchase price and he was also well pleased to get rid of the vicious animal. The syndicate which had purchased him was equally pleased to get such an unrideable horse. There would be rare competition now at the shows with such a wild horse to be ridden.

All the rodeo horses were well looked after, for they were, after all, an investment, but special care was taken with the red colt. He was treated with immense respect and no man or groom ever allowed himself in with him unless the animal was fastened by ropes.

This was all so confusing to Jago that to start with he did not fight or threaten anybody at all and the syndicate chiefs wondered uneasily if they had been fooled. Jago allowed himself to be roped without fuss or bother, he made not the slightest attempt to savage anyone, and because, as yet, they had not produced a saddle, his behaviour was almost exemplary.

One hot afternoon he was driven with the aid of cracking whips down a long, tall, wooden lane, just wide enough for him to move, and branching off to the left. Jago turned cautiously down the branch, wondering uneasily what all this was about. He was bothered and worried because the men's noises were getting even louder. Quite suddenly he came up against a wooden obstruction but before he could back away rails dropped behind and he was trapped.

Jago reared, trying to reach over the top rail, but it was too high; he could go neither back nor forward and now he started to get angry. Yet again he had been betrayed.

His anger turned to burning rage when the men, bending over the top rail, dropped the heavy saddle on his back and pulled the girth up under his belly; but try as he might, Jago found it was quite impossible to reach them with his teeth.

They pulled a blindfold over his head to force a bitless bridle on his mouth and while he stood in frozen horror, they retightened the girth and the extra safety strap which ensured that the saddle never slipped.

A long rope went from the head collar and it was on to this that the rider could hold, but only with one hand. His other must be kept free, away from person or saddle. If he touched either, he was disqualified; he had to stay in the saddle ten seconds and would then be taken off to safety by mounted riders in the large ring.

Jago knew nothing of this. All he did know was that a man meant to get on his back again and this thought was enough to make his temper boil. Once that blindfold was removed and this obstruction taken away, he would show the man.

The chosen rider slowly climbed the rails, all the time eyeing the red colt—a stranger on the buckjumping circuit—trying to fathom the depth of the horse's temper. He wondered what this one would be like. Did he buck, kick, and rear, or did he have his own fancy pattern of explosive behaviour? This red colt, this Jago, was an unknown quantity but *he* was the champion rider for the State of Queensland and he was pleased at having drawn the first ride on the unknown red colt.

Delicately he lowered himself into the saddle while on either side of the rails men held the colt steady. The man settled himself down, gripped, anchored his feet in the stirrups, took the rope in his left hand and a deep breath at the same time.

The barrier moved and Jago shot out bucking wildly, hooves leaving the ground three or four feet high. He felt the rider's strength so without further preamble he braked to a halt in the middle of the show ring, and started his see-sawing movements, rearing high then dropping down and kicking in a vertical line. He did this four times in rapid succession then whipped round in a tight little circle, bucking hard, back humped, hooves smashing the dust.

Jago felt the rider loosening; one more vicious circle of plunges and he hurtled into the air. Jago went on kicking then spinning around, and finally reversed in his tracks to attack the rider; but he was too late, he was already safely double-banked on another horse.

It had been so easy! Jago galloped down to the end of the show ground seeking an exit and, finding none, careered on around the perimeter chased by a mounted stockman, who taking advantage of Jago's excitement, roped him and took him back to the chutes.

Jago was still excited as he was forced back into the small, high-railed stall. What was going to happen now? He stood in a white lather of sweat, his eyes rolling, warning the men not to put their hands through the rails. In a way he was exhilarated at the ease with which he had thrown the rider but he was also frustrated that he had been unable to catch and hurt him. It was obvious that as soon as a man was thrown, he must turn immediately and hurtle into an attack.

Such was Jago's hatred of men by this stage that it showed

itself in an aura and men stared uneasily at him, wondering just what had happened to make a horse hate men so much.

Many horses dislike men but there is a vast difference between dislike and outright hate: there was no mistaking the fact that the red colt loathed the sight of all men.

Later on Jago was ridden again and the rider who drew him, having watched the earlier episode, was uneasy as he settled in the saddle.

"Make sure those pick-ups are quick off the mark!" he yelled to an official.

Stamping his feet, Jago tensed as the weight slid into the saddle. Impatiently he half reared, striking at the barrier, anxious to get out into the ring.

The barrier lifted and before he was out of the chute Jago was bucking, once, twice, then his see-saw movement, completed by the vicious, cruel, bucking circle, which was practically impossible to sit.

The rider was falling, falling, he was off! Jago flew round on the spot, rearing in his haste and preparing to charge, but the riders were even quicker. A whip cracked in warning, Jago ignored it, and the lash bit his shoulders. In rage he turned to make a different attack but he could not face the cutting whip. By the time he had dodged to evade the rider, the thrown horseman was half-way out of the ring, again double-banked. Jago flew after him, galloping at his top speed, the crowd shouting in amazement. They had never seen such a pace outside the race-track. Excited, they stood shouting and cheering at the red horse. As the gate crashed in his face Jago sullenly swung aside to race around again, seeking some other escape—anything rather than the ropes around his neck.

He was in such a fury that for once he forgot his earlier lessons; digging in his toes, he shook his head, trying to break the ropes by sheer strength, but as they started hurting him he darted forward, determined to knock at least one horse to the ground. The riders nimbly drove their animals at angles, to right and left, and Jago was forced to halt. Rearing high, he squealed not so much in challenge as in despair.

All he wanted was to be free, to roam wild, to have nothing at all to do with men, but no matter where he galloped and searched there was no exit, only the ropes, hauling him back to the tight little cage, to the fresh rider, to the roars from the crowd.

Again Jago screeched and then stood still for three seconds. Flaring his nostrils, he tried desperately to pick up some scent which would remind him of those weeks spent roaming the bushland as leader. But there was nothing, only the scents of men, men, and more men.

He lowered his head, flopped his ears forward dolefully, feeling for the first time in his life great sadness. Then the ropes pulled, this feeling vanished, and he was all anger and hate again as the riders dragged him back ready for another event.

He was more than a prisoner of men; he was a victim of his own hate. If he could have bent to the men's will, life might have been a little easier, but Jago was like an iron convict. He could not, he would not, yield his spirit and will to the dictates of men.

He hated too much.

CHAPTER SIX

The Red Devil

THEY forgot the name Jago which Mike Colston had handed on from Peter Huston. He became known instead as the Red Devil. The fiend incarnate of the rodeo circuit. The horse which the buckjump riders dreaded drawing.

For a whole year Jago was used as a rodeo horse travelling around the vast continent until he became as well known as the Melbourne Cup winner himself. To the syndicate, he was a valuable attraction. People turned up just to watch the Red Devil alone, to see if anyone could ride him for the required time, and, more morbidly, to see if the red horse could ever catch his thrown rider.

Jago tried every time and the continual failures did nothing to improve a temper which was as savage now as that of a starving caged leopard. He was totally unpredictable and positively vicious. Even the men who fed him treated him with kid gloves and whenever the red horse was moved anywhere, ropes were around his neck and a rifle was cradled in someone's arm.

The men had soon found out that Jago was frightened of a rifle. They used this knowledge for their own safety. They had no wish to shoot the horse, he was far too valuable to them, but they dare not risk his killing any person, and there was not the slightest doubt in anyone's mind that given the tiniest opportunity the Red Devil would kill.

Two or three well-meaning people attempted to win him

over with kindness, with tit-bits of foods, with soft words and pats on the neck—through the rails—but kindness from man had come far too late.

Jago was suspicious of anything from man. He even examined his food carefully. Man had played so many horrible tricks that nothing about him could be trusted. Two of these kindly people paid for their pains. They laughed at the warnings, persisted, and were well and truly bitten.

While Jago had always been a hard horse to ride, he was now quite impossible. No rider succeeded in staying on him for the requisite time though many tried hard. As his fame and notoriety grew, men came from all over the country to try and ride the red horse, but he beat them all. He had developed a routine which started as soon as a man sat on his back in the chute. Once the weight was in his saddle Jago would begin the fight without bothering to wait for the barrier to go. He would half rear and plunge and he had now learned it was possible to crush the rider's legs against the rails of the chute. The second the barrier was released, Jago would shoot out, a whirlwind of vicious action. Quite often he had deposited his rider before they had gone two yards from the barrier and only rarely did man and horse reach the centre of the showground.

Jago's peculiar and highly distinctive see-saw movements became his trademark. If a rider stuck with him as far as this action then the crowd considered him very good indeed but few were able to stay in the saddle for Jago's bucking circle. This move was almost impossible to sit. The rider would lose his balance and, no matter how strong his grip, without balance he was lost. Many men found themselves falling through sheer dizziness and it was astonishing how the horse kept his own sense of equilibrium.

Jago never wasted time in straight bucking. He knew it was a waste of effort and could easily be ridden by experienced men, but the see-sawing, the bucking circle, always removed them. If even that failed, he would try his trump card—the terrible, deliberate fall which had ruined Warrigan's life.

Only twice did he have to try this and each time the crowd had risen in horror. His action had been performed in such deliberate cold blood that men began saying the Red Devil could think, which was of course nonsense. No animal has man's reasoning ability. No animal has an imaginative mind— man is supreme in this respect. But Jago did have his superior intelligence and this, coupled with his hate, gave him the ability to try, by experiment, the most cunning ways of removing a rider.

A less clever horse would have used so many moves and left it at that. Jago was sharp, quick in action, and filled with diabolical cunning, and it was this, as much as anything, that made him dangerous. For although he had this routine, this dancing, fighting repertoire, a rider was never wholly sure what else the horse might try. He was unpredictable.

Jago remembered a number of things, mostly those which he could associate with his past life. He never consciously thought about his days as a racehorse but one special Saturday he did remember them.

The horse pens had been sited to one side of the showground giving a clear view of the events as they took place. Memories of his racing days flooded back to Jago as he watched the trotting races. He had never worn any type of harness, he had not been broken to sulky or gig, but the trotters and pacers were thoroughbreds like himself. The preparation, the parading, the general excitement from the crowd, pushed his memories forward in his brain.

He even became a little nostalgic because he loved to extend his legs in a fast gallop and this he had not done since becoming a rodeo horse. He craved his freedom, he wanted it more than anything else—more even than food; just to know again the sheer joy of galloping wildly over flat ground. Here he was nothing but a prisoner. Because of his reputation he was kept confined, and exercised himself, when not at the shows, in small, high-railed yards. This was not enough for his spirit. He was like a prisoner in gaol, yearning, breaking his heart, for a free, wild life.

He would stand in solitary state, whinnying and screeching his misery over the night air. His clever head would be continually lifting and moving as he hopefully tried to find the tiniest tell-tale scent of his beloved bush, and always failing, his spirits would sink, his temper would become more savage, until Jago really did become a Red Devil.

He was now a fully-grown horse, standing just over sixteen hands. His body was lean with the muscles running in hard curves over his frame, the legs were of iron. No horse had such legs. Even after a year as a buckjumper, they were still free from blemishes. No splints or spavins, no galls or curbs, which was entirely due to his fine breeding. Many of the other horses succumbed; their legs could not stand the continual strain from thrashing the hard ground in violent leaps. On Jago, however, there was only one scar where the rifle bullet had ploughed a furrow on his shoulder. The hair had grown over this scar lighter in colour and from a distance this was most noticeable; a pink streak against the flaming red.

Jago was even more beautiful now that he had attained his full growth, and all men admired him. The perfectly made horse is as rare as the perfect man but Jago stood out in a class of his own. His beauty was only marred by the ugly look in his eyes, in the way he opened his jaws and threatened with his large teeth, and in the tiny ears always laid back in anger. It was rare to see his ears pricked forward in interest.

All people knew him, all admired him, and many felt pity that he was as he was. His history was common knowledge now and many harsh words were said, perhaps unfairly, about Bereeba Station and its owner, Mike Colston.

Jago was fated to turn out as he was, if not sooner then certainly later. He was born a rogue. As a racehorse he had hated the saddle, and even with kindness his true temper would have revealed itself as he matured. His treatment by Warrigan had only hastened the inevitable.

As Jago hated, as he yearned for his freedom, so he wanted something else. He wanted to kill a man.

The instinct to kill is prevalent in many wild animals. Lions, tigers, leopards, wolves, all have this blood-lust because they are carnivorous. A leopard will kill for sheer fun as will the English red fox. But a horse is a herbivorous animal. He never eats flesh and, fortunately for man, the horse who wants to kill is extremely rare.

Jago did not want to kill for food; his feelings were solely revengeful. But his yearning to pound and trample a man beneath his wicked hooves never abated; rather it grew as the weeks turned into months. He tried hard enough but luckily the riders in the showgrounds were highly efficient. They never failed to pick up the thrown rider in time, and armed with long whips they were able to keep at bay the furious red horse.

Although Jago's wildness was hereditary, his yearning to kill arose solely because of his treatment. Any other horse would have been angry, would have fought in the ring, but would not necessarily have turned to killer.

The men who handled him talked uneasily about his behaviour, wondering why it was so. They did not understand that some animals cannot bear continuous solitary confinement. All Jago wanted was his freedom, and this, his greatest wish, was denied.

They had tried turning him loose with some of the other horses but he promptly fought them, establishing himself as leader and damaging other valuable rodeo horses. They found too that when loose with others he was more difficult and dangerous to catch, even with ropes.

At the end of the year, when the horses were to be sent for rest, the problem of Jago arose. The rodeo men discussed him anxiously. They dare not turn him loose with other horses, nor could he be free near men. Was it perhaps not better to get rid of him? His temper was so savage, his reputation now so tarnished with hate, that riders were afraid of him. They were terrified in case he caught them helpless on the ground, panic-stricken at the thought of facing the Red Devil. His appeal was waning, and where once the public loved him for beating men, now they were too afraid. As a security risk he was useless. It only wanted one inquisitive boy to climb the rails as a dare, and they would have a killing on their hands.

To reform him was out of the question. He was past reforming and anyhow, what man would want to tackle such a challenge? With great reluctance they decided that the Red Devil was no more use to them. They took this decision only now that their actions and useage had made him even more wicked. What Mike Colston and Warrigan had started, they had completed.

The sufferer was the red horse.

The decision was unanimous. He must be shot.

Jago, of course, had no knowledge of this but he did have his instincts. As the dog to be drowned in a sack can sense impending doom, so did Jago suddenly realize that the men who fed and handled him had a different scent about their persons. They were still afraid of him, they were still cautious and respectful, but their attitude was subtly different.

He could sense, with irrefutable clarity, danger and death to himself. He never relaxed a second once he felt this; even at night, when resting, he would awaken very quickly and look around, testing the breeze, listening and scenting, then he would briefly sleep again.

They moved him back up to Queensland where the other horses could be rested in long, open paddocks, and at a small place, a long way from where people might see, they decided to kill the Red Devil. They knew their action would bring forth an uproar from a public which was all too quick to change sides but they had the excuse of an attack ready.

Jago never knew that the death sentence was to be carried out the next day. His fears had somewhat diminished. They had put him in a small, railed paddock, given him water and feed, and left him for the night. But Jago did not eat. He was too tensed and excited.

Way out there was the wonderful, fascinating bushland. He could smell it, he could hear it, he could sense it, but how to get there?

He roamed the paddock, now and again stopping to lean his weight against the rails, but they were too firmly trenched into the ground. He turned his attention to the gate through which he had been driven, but not only was the latch firmly in its socket, the gate was also padlocked. Irritated, unhappy, and at the same time wildly excited Jago prowled the paddock like an angry lion in a cage at the zoo.

He was so near to freedom but how to reach it?

He broke into a sharp canter, circling the paddock, hunting for an exit. Finding none he halted, turned, and stared at the rails. They were tremendously solid and very high, certainly higher than Jago had ever jumped before and higher than most horses could leap at all except perhaps the highly trained show jumper.

But Jago was no jumper: he had been bred for speed and nothing else. He could manage an ordinary jump but the tall, solid poles frightened him. He knew that if he jumped and made a mistake his own legs would be hurt and for a time he resisted the call of the bush.

But as the night wore on, the urge for freedom grew stronger and Jago became more agitated. Three times he cantered up to the rails and three times he swerved aside at the last moment, his nerve failing him. When dawn broke, it was an angry, restless horse who greeted the day; a horse whose heart was breaking with longing, whose spirit was at its lowest ebb, who could easily have lain down and died if he had been a quitter.

Jago needed an impetus. He could not tackle the jump in cold blood, no horse could, but if something, some new urge was presented, he would attempt it.

The incentive was coming though he did not realize it. But when the sun started skidding over the early morning sky and Jago saw the two men, his heart started rapping with fright. Only too clearly he saw and recognized the terrible rifles under the men's arms. Only too well now did he understand the death scent on the men. They were coming for him, and against rifles he was as helpless as a day-old foal. He dare not stand and fight the booming stick.

Jago careered around the paddock again in an absolute frenzy of fear and impatience. He had to be free, he must get away from the armed men, and he had to do it now. There would never be another chance.

Without hesitation he swung round and charged at the rails. With every stride he increased his speed until he had never moved so fast. The rails loomed up, horribly tall and solid. Jago pressed with his hocks and flung himself up, clawing for the blue sky, his freedom, and his life. Only a desperate horse would have attempted such a leap.

His red head and neck were outstretched and his front legs as straight in front as possible. He flung himself horizontal, his tail out like a flag, his hind legs with the bunching quarters also horizontal.

His front hooves cleared the top rail by an inch and then he was dropping downward. One hind leg cleared but the other caught, the fetlock catching around the top rail. Jago felt the obstruction, he felt his collected descent faltering, and suddenly he was falling. He hit the ground with a crump, rolled over twice with his own momentum, and lay still for a second, winded, shocked, and horrified.

Then the shouting men's voices hit his ears. The peril was getting closer and frantically he scrambled erect and hurled himself into a fast gallop, the pain from the fetlock forgotten in his feverish desire to flee from the armed men.

A rifle boomed and a bullet swished past his head. Again it boomed and the second bullet parted the hairs on his off-side quarters. Burning with heat, its power spent, it dropped on to the ground.

The rifle sounds, the bullet's pain, spurred Jago into even faster action. He had never galloped quite so fast as he did that morning in making his break for freedom.

All the time his ears were back, listening to the sounds behind. He knew the men had quickly mounted their horses and he knew also that their deadly rifles were still trained his way.

Jago swerved, his instincts in command again, and another bullet missed him entirely. Thrashing over the flat bushland, winding in and out of trees, Jago fled for his life. He hurtled down a long, crumbling slope, nearly slipping and rolling in his haste to get to the bottom, then there was the heart-rending scramble up the far side. On again, hooves thrashing and leaving a cloud of dust in his trail. He veered down a dry river bed, his feet skidding off rocks and shale, then up the bank and off again over flat land. Dry, brown, and dusty, it went on and on into the horizon where in the vague distance, just poking delicate fingers into the sky, stood a range of low mountains.

Jago drove himself as he had never allowed a jockey to drive him. His pace never decreased for one stride. The year as a rodeo horse had toughened his body to a remarkable degree; otherwise he would have collapsed, beaten and blown.

His nostrils were wide open for maximum intake of air and the red membranes were vivid, merging in with the red hair of his body. Sweat was rolling down his neck and shoulders and trickling down his flanks. His eyes were wild with fear and effort, continually looking backwards, estimating the distance between himself and the riders. His ears only came forward when he jumped small obstacles, dodged under low branches, or slithered down and up river banks.

His heart pounded in his own ears, a dull, quickening *boom, boom*, but his great rib cavity stood the strain. His lungs expanded and deflated as they consumed the oxygen and turned it into blood for the ever-demanding heart.

This organ screamed for power; it had to drive the iron legs and keep the massive hocks propelling the large body; it had to feed the muscles and tendons, it had to flow into the brain so that the instructions to the nerves were not delayed by slow reflexes. Jago's heart had never been given such demanding work but it was a good heart, well up to the effort required of it, and it was a game heart too; for sustaining it was the red horse's mighty spirit, his desire to live as he wanted. The inherited wildness of the rogue had lain dormant for one reason only: to come out again in a true wild horse, not a pampered product of soft stables and green grass.

Nature had brought this majestic mixture together in the one animal, but to use it he must be free and wild. Nature will only help so much. She will make an opportunity available, but it is up to the animal—or man—to use it. If Jago had faltered, hesitated, or refused that jump, there would have been no further chance.

He galloped on, not tiring in the least. A desperate animal does not know fatigue. All Jago knew was that the riders were still on his tail. They were dropping further and further away but they were still there. He had to keep going until he could stand and sleep without the fear of the man scent creeping up on him.

As Jago flew onward he never ceased looking alertly ahead. Once before he had galloped like this and men had been waiting for him in ambush. He did not forget, he constantly scanned every tree and shrub, every shadow and rise, to ascertain that it was free from the dreadful man.

The riders, meanwhile, were in a panic! This horse was

leaving them standing. A killer horse roaming the open bush
—the very thought of it appalled them! They spurred their
failing horses but they knew their chance was lessening. How
could anything hope to catch up with that red horse unless he
had wings and an engine?

Their horses started to falter. They were not bred for such
effort or speed, nor did they have the red horse's drive for life
or freedom.

The riders had to pull their mounts up and get out of the
saddles to loosen the girths. Their horses stood, heads hanging
low, blowing uneasily, beaten by the effort.

"Well, that's done it!" said one.

"What a jump!"

"If he meets anyone, though, he'll kill them!"

"There's no one out there. Only dust and heat. He'll never
stand it. He's not bred for the wild. Give him a week and he'll
be dead."

"Perhaps we should send a plane up—"

"For a horse? You're crazy!"

"My horse is done, I'm going back!"

They mounted, settling themselves gently in their saddles.
The red horse had certainly beaten them. Who would have
thought any horse could jump such high rails? It was fantastic,
it was incredible, and it was to become one more tale that
would grow up round the legend of the great red horse.

They turned and left, their dust cloud getting smaller, but
behind them, in the opposite direction, Jago still galloped on.

All other horses would have at least slackened their pace by
now and perhaps even halted altogether to stare back at the
retreating enemy, but not Jago.

Men had fooled him so many times in the past that he refused to believe what his eyes saw. The men were riding away, but men were cunning. This could be just the prelude to some other action, some other trap to catch him. He went on heading forward, legs sweeping backward and forward until they were a red blur. His action was easy as well as fast, his hooves never faltered on earth or shale. His heart and lungs were working efficiently and were nowhere near failing.

Jago galloped on all that morning and if there had been men to see his progress, their story would not have been believed. It is thought impossible for a horse to gallop hour after hour in a straight line, but Jago did this very thing.

He covered the flat, dull, and uninteresting plain and was steadily driving himself nearer the low mountains. His coat was no longer red. Sweat had formed a white lather and now even this had been washed off to be replaced by black wetness. Even his tail was dripping and his mane flopped limply in a damp mass, tumbling over both sides of his neck. The wild look had gone from his eyes; instead they burned with the gleam of the fanatic. He had been galloping so long and so far that his heart and lungs had almost forgotten there was any other pace.

And still he galloped onward.

He was an incredible machine of nerves, tendons, sinews, and muscles, and the engine was the spirit. The fine, indomitable, uncomplaining spirit of the beautiful thoroughbred horse. As long as the nostrils could flare in the oxygen, then the lungs could drive like bellows, the heart could pound the blood forward with the great valves opening and shutting in quick, regular rhythm, and the legs could stamp down with the strong hocks hurling the great body ever onward.

The mountains loomed nearer and still the horse galloped on. He had been travelling for nearly four hours now, a fantastic time for a horse to gallop of his own accord, but Jago's feelings, like his experiences, were exceptional.

Amongst other things, his instinct was telling him to keep going, to put every possible stride between himself and the men. The low mountains would provide safety in the form of cover. There he could hide and rest, but not here, not now. He must go on and even faster!

Stride after powerful stride smashed over the rock-hard earth in almost effortless precision and it was only as the mountains loomed near and details stood out with clarity, that the legs slowed their pace a fraction.

Jago studied the scene before him. The brown slopes going up into the sky seemed enormous to him who had never seen such sharp, high peaks—different entirely from the land in Victoria which, although high, was tree-covered. Jago looked ahead. Rocks he could see, earth, some stunted trees, and everything a dull brown.

Everywhere, too, there was thick dust—brown dust, pale white dust—and it was this that started catching at his throat. He had sweated so much without drinking all night that he was getting near the point of dehydration. Very soon he would have to stop for water, but where on that arid mountain face was there water?

As the riders had so bluntly said, this was the wild bush where death was commonplace and he was the pampered thoroughbred. How could a horse like Jago hope to survive in such a cruel place?

Nature had given him his chance: he had taken it and had made the jump. She would give him no other. If he wanted to survive, he would have to work for it.

CHAPTER SEVEN

Living Wild

THE sun was at its peak when Jago broke back into a trot to scramble amongst the white, sun-bleached rocks at the foot of the mountains. He wove his way along a narrow, almost indiscernible, track and finally dropped back to a walk.

He had never imagined such heat. The lowland at the foot of the mountain acted as a trap. The sun's rays landed there from early morning until late afternoon and always the air was oven hot; the temperature never fell below a hundred degrees and to a sweaty horse after a four-hour gallop it was almost too much to bear.

Jago plodded on. His senses told him this was no place to stop, rest, and reconnoitre the situation. He pressed forward, seeking shade, hoping to find water.

After another two hours' walking he did find his shade. Breasting a slope he saw a clump of trees hugging each other. Everything was still and quiet, the only sounds being Jago's own hooves rattling on stones and rocks, the screeching of the odd cricket, and the sound that heat makes when it bounces off hot stone.

He scrambled down and stood under the trees, his ears pricked at this great unknown, this vast emptiness, and once his senses had satisfied him that he really was alone, he relaxed a little and rested.

Now that he had stopped moving he realized just how tired he was. The energy which his body had used in his wild gallop was incredible and he was much thinner than when he made the jump for freedom. The sweat had caked into a salty layer on his coat, and the sun's rays, poking through the branches, twinkled as they lit on the dried crystals.

It took his body a long time to cool down and until it did Jago stood immobile. Once he would have looked like some great statue carved from stone but now he was as ragged-looking and disreputable as the lowest wild horse.

The white dust had settled on his wet coat and his true colour was invisible. His head hung low while waves of fatigue washed through his limbs. As his body cooled the fetlock started to ache; it had been severely twisted when caught on the top rail and now it began to swell.

But the cruellest hardship was thirst. Jago had experienced many terrible things in his life but all the past pains were nothing compared to this desperate yearning for water. It was not just a natural thirst after abstention but the screaming of his body tissues for water to restock his body with liquid again.

He had to drink soon or die. But he was not a wild horse. He did not know how to look for water, or where. He had received no training from his dam in this respect. Always before when he had been thirsty men had provided the water.

But nature must have pitied the proud, exhausted horse and, breaking her inflexible rule, given him just a little more assistance. As evening drew blue and black shadows over the mountains, a slight breeze arose and on it Jago smelt water.

He was instantly alert, head high, trying to locate the faint scent. The breeze flickered again then dropped. He had been given his chance, now it was up to him.

Jago stood, hesitant and unsure, but aware that he must drink or die. It was an effort to think about moving, to push one weary leg forward and start the chain reaction that became a slow, shambling walk, but Jago did it where nine other horses out of ten would have failed. He did it because his will to live, now that he had his precious freedom, was stronger than any other thing. It over-rode the fatigue, the aches, the pain from the fetlock; his will and spirit were invincible.

He was limping badly as he struggled towards where he thought the precious water lay. He was not wholly sure of the direction and if he was wrong, then die he certainly would.

But his quick senses had made no error. His direction was correct, though to reach the water was a heart-breaking struggle where every hesitant, wobbly step needed as much energy as the fierce gallop.

Jago was very near the end of his tether but he did not know this. All he knew was that somewhere there was water, and this he must have. It took him a whole hour to find the water and his progress down the rock and shale slope was pitiful.

The fetlock was so swollen now that little weight could be put on the joint and in a queer, three-legged, hopping motion Jago slithered his gaunt body down to the tiniest of water holes lying between two large, white rocks.

The water came from an underground spring which only broke the surface at this one point. It was good water, clean and sweet, but it only flowed slowly. Around its little hole green grass sprouted for a yard in either direction before giving way to the rock and sun and dust.

Jago struggled to the water, lowered his head, and plunged his nose into the sweet coolness. Never before had that common drink, water, been so luxuriously refreshing.

He wanted to suck great gulps of the cold fire down his parched throat but the spring flowed too slowly, which was just as well. If Jago had drunk fast and excessively he would only have given himself colic. He had to wait, take his time, drink gently. It was another hour before his body was satisfied and only then did he lower his head to snap hungrily at the little circle of green grass.

Once the thirst had been quenched, came hunger, but the small patch of grass would not have satisfied a Shetland pony, let alone a large horse after a morning's galloping. But what little there was helped and by the time the moon had come up Jago was standing against the spring, resting and re-charging his batteries.

He stood there all night, now and again opening both eyes to look around. Now that he was in the wild he started behaving like a wild animal. He had never been taught this, it was just the old hereditary instinct working again. His ears were never still, but continually flickering one way or another, listening and identifying the sounds, ascertaining what they were, where they were, and whether they were coming nearer.

Many of the sounds were foreign to him on that first night of freedom because although he had roamed wild and free in the paddock so long ago at Bereeba, this was the bush proper; and Jago had much to learn if he wished to survive.

In the morning he could not move if he had wanted to. The fetlock joint was now so swollen that no weight at all could be taken on the limb and Jago stood limply, the leg hovering just above the ground.

He spent that day drinking, resting, and waiting for his leg to mend. In that fatalistic way of all horses he made no sound of complaint. He uttered no cry but just stood, patient and still weary.

In fact it was a whole week before weight could be placed on the fetlock joint and by this time Jago's position was again desperate. He had been with water all this time but of food he had had none. The small patch of grass was long since exhausted and in desperation, Jago struggled back up the slope to the cluster of trees and gnawed at the bark. Chewing what he had bitten off, he found that this was no help to his stomach.

Once, he would have been fussy in the extreme about what he ate but now he would try anything. He rooted at the base of the trees, pulling up the tiny wisps of brown grass which hopefully tried to grow there, and then he limped away from the trees, searching for something, anything, to chew and swallow; anything to drive away the griping pains in his belly. But there was nothing.

The land around the base of the mountains was too harsh and inhospitable for anything to grow or live. The heat was too extreme. No plant could survive in that baking oven. Rain had not fallen in years though Jago was not to know this. Only the little spring faithfully tumbled out to splash in silver curtseys between the two rocks before it disappeared underground to some deep, hidden reservoir.

At last it penetrated into Jago's head that he would have to move and find food; if he left it any longer he would be too weak. But where was the water out there? This precious little pool was as valuable to him as the most priceless diamond to a miner.

Finally his stomach drove him away. With slow and often hesitant steps he moved away from the pool which had saved his life. It was up to him now to sustain himself.

How he managed to live during the next few weeks was a small miracle. He had no knowledge of the bush, no inherited intuition, and every move he made was a struggle, a learning from trial and error.

He ranged far and wide, searching for grass fit to eat, and always he was driven back to the water hole to drink. He became even leaner and harder and learned to do without water for longer periods than before.

But the struggle was heart-breaking and soul-destroying. Only Jago could have survived it all. The day came, however, when he had eaten everything in the area. He would now have to go further afield and this meant the journeys back for water would get longer and longer.

In a way this was a good thing. It took him out more into the open bushland. Being patient and determined he did find other food. It took him every hour of daylight to get enough to keep his great body going, and on fare which once he would have scorned, but all the time he was learning.

He discovered which grasses made better feed than others. Some he could eat all day and still feel hungry while others were more nourishing. But the grass was scattered over a wider area and it was only where the sun failed to shine on it directly that it was able to grow. In the boiling heat nothing could live.

And so one morning Jago reluctantly left the area. With a springy trot he pushed out into the great unknown. It was a gamble because wherever he went it was essential that he find water.

The first night he was unlucky. There was water but he did not know how to find it. He was standing upon yet another dried-up river bed. Thin, brackish water still seeped through the ground and with pawing he could have unearthed enough liquid to refresh himself but the thought of digging for water did not occur to him. Why should it? A horse is not a mole and the horse untrained to the bush is quite as helpless as a man on a raft at sea without the equipment to live off plankton.

The next morning Jago's thirst pushed hunger away and the first search was for another water hole. It was too far to go back to his first discovery; he would only leave his bones to bleach as a memorial.

He wandered around like a lost soul in torment and by night his thirst was driving him crazy. Sullenly he came back to the dried river bed and stood in agony scraping a hoof in his agitation. Why he started pawing he never knew; it was not thought or reason or even memory, but some trace of instinct from long-dead ancestors. He felt he had to dig and so the hoof kept striking downward. Its movement was slow and shallow with weakness but the instinct kept urging him on.

A dog has no thought or reason for burying a bone but it knows it must do this. Neither does a dog understand why it must circle two or three times before it lies down at night. In both cases, it is ancient wild instinct which has been carried down through countless generations. The dog buries his bone to rot the meat, and as a store, and he turns around to make sure no snakes or other creatures are lying in his chosen bed.

So it was with Jago. Deeply-hidden instincts were rising now that he was a free, wild animal. He continued to dig and scrape then changed over to use the other hoof. His thirst was so acute that his tongue was starting to swell. Unless he had liquid soon it would thicken, go black, and he would soon die.

Jago became slower and slower as his weakness increased until suddenly his ears shot forward in deep interest. His heart gave an extra-large pound and he quickened his scraping, working with concentration now. The shale had given way to soil—poor, barren stuff but it was now damp. As Jago dug, the dampness spread as in a sponge, and very gradually, in his tiny little hole, moisture began to form.

He lowered his head and impatiently tried to suck some liquid but more work was needed first. He started scraping more quickly. Water was all he could think of. Even his man-hate had been forgotten in his urge and craving to drink. He could smell the water, tangy and brackish but nevertheless water.

Nearly eighteen inches down the water started seeping through. It gradually filtered up and collected in a tiny, dirty puddle. Jago lowered his head and drank, ignoring the smell and taste. Once he would have refused such water, but he was no longer the pampered, fastidious racehorse. He was the wild animal, fighting to survive.

It took him nearly all night to drink his fill. He had to keep scraping with his hooves, encouraging the water to flow, then drinking quickly what had collected.

By morning, he was refreshed though his thirst was not fully quenched, and he had learned another valuable lesson: that even in the vast, cruel dead heart of Australia there is water, if you work to find it.

Only a few animals know this, only a few have the wit and will to seek out and dig for life, and those that don't must die. The wandering tribes of aborigines know all the water holes, and to the first white settlers it was remarkable and uncanny how they could live and cross a burning waste, while the weak, civilized whites fell and died.

So it was with Jago.

He would often be thirsty again, he would have to work to find his water, but he would never actually die of thirst now and in his lonely wanderings he always located, if not water at least a place which might yield it to the striking hoof.

Revived, he turned to his other pressing need for food, and so it went on. The eternal cycle of the wild animal. Food, drink, and a mate. Jago had no time for the last. He was too busy learning how to survive.

His days were spent scavenging for food, his evenings in locating water, and at night he always stayed by his precious water. He roamed far and wide in the months that followed, slowly building up his body and extending his knowledge of the wild life.

He left the hills behind and moved ever onward, exploring, eating, and drinking. Not once did he see a man, but then he was not to know that men had no use for this land. It could not raise stock, it was useless for crops, and so they ignored it, interested only if at any time it might yield up precious metals.

Jago crossed from one state to another but that meant nothing to him either. He had adapted himself to this wild life with amazing ease and for perhaps the first time in his life he was remarkably happy.

Just as some men, no matter what they have done, can never be incarcerated in prison and remain sane, so there are some animals who will never be chained to the discipline of man's will. Jago was a rare specimen. He had to be free. He could contemplate nothing else.

As the months passed he began to forget about the twelve hard months as a rodeo horse; there was nothing here to remind him of them, no tamed horse, no man, no rifle or rope. Without the association, the memories disappeared, giving place to the primeval demands of sheer living.

As he became used to his wild life and learned how to live

off the land, Jago began to feel lonely. The horse is a gregarious animal. As a herd-dweller it is unnatural for him to be a hermit and so Jago was now constantly on the lookout for his own kind.

One never to be forgotten day he actually did catch a horse-scent on the evening breeze and his first impulse was to scream out a greeting. Then his instincts cautioned against such reckless folly and with guile he headed silently towards the scent, approaching downwind, moving like a wraith. When he was very near he caught the unmistakable tang of a man and abruptly he shied away in sudden fright. All his terrible memories coming back to him and the lone jackeroo never knew, as he made his evening camp, that a pair of eyes was watching him, filled with a mixture of fright and hate.

As silently as he came, Jago left. He wanted nothing to do with any tamed horse and once out of earshot he sprang into a sharp canter and put as much distance as possible between himself and his enemy.

Here again, his new-found instincts came into force. He did not just gallop wildly as he would once have done, without thought of where he was going. Now he was all fierce cunning and he cantered only over the hardest ground where his tracks would be practically impossible to follow. No-one had taught him this, no-one had even demonstrated it; this was just another instance of centuries-old instinct working when civilization has been discarded.

Jago never went near that part of the country again; he moved on to fresh lands. One night something was different. He did not know what it was, so, uneasily, he kept himself awake and alert, scenting the air, straining his ears and continually looking around.

He did not think to look up at the sky because horses are not inclined to look upwards like cats or monkeys. But if he had done so, he would have seen that rare sight in the dry outback—foaming clouds pushed along by a brisk wind.

It was this wind which had alerted Jago to something being different. With the rain-clouds the dust settled, the crickets became silent, the birds and flies vanished as the land held its breath for the blessed rain.

So often these rain-clouds had passed over taking their precious loads elsewhere when the bush was crying with thirst. A raindrop reluctantly plopped down from the dark sky and disappeared in the dust. Another followed in exactly the same place and without any further warning the rain began to pour down.

Water came cascading down in a gigantic shower. Thunder rolled and lightning tore the sky as the clouds writhed.

Jago stood in fascinated awe, not in the least frightened. He thought the downpour of water one of the most marvellous spectacles he had ever witnessed. It was the first time since leaving the racing stables that his coat had been cleaned. All the accumulated dust and sweat was washed from between his red hairs and the feeling of cleanliness was luxurious.

He slowly crumpled at the hocks and indulged in the joy of a roll. Kicking and stretching his legs like an ungainly yearling, then lumbering to his feet, he shook himself all over and stood with head low, allowing the raindrops to lash his body clean.

The storm did not last for long but the next morning, as the sun arose, everything—including Jago—steamed. On such a morning it was good to be alive, and in sheer high spirits, Jago bucked a couple of times then reared high, greeting the freshly-washed sky.

With the brief rain-shower life sprang to the land. Only a brief life but enough to show what could happen if water were always present.

Seeds, which had lain dormant for months and sometimes years, burst forth swollen with water. Tiny hair-roots hastily sank themselves to drink greedily while the chance was there. Bright-coloured flowers preened themselves in brief glory. The birds sang sweeter, the crickets burst forth into a harmonious rhapsody of living, and the whole bush seethed with sound and happiness.

And no living being was happier than the great red horse. He had food and water in plenty. What more could he want?

He wanted companionship.

That this was denied him was pure bad luck. There are many herds of wild brumby horses roaming the Australian Continent and Jago had been unfortunate. In his roaming he had never crossed their wandering paths. All he saw were the natural wild animals. The kangaroos and wallabies, the wombats and possums, the bandicoots and snakes, and of course, the dingoes, the wild Australian dogs which roam in small packs and which are the bane of the sheep farmer's life.

Jago neither liked nor disliked the dingo—his feelings were totally neutral—but after months spent roaming with no companionship from other horses he began to look upon the dingoes with a more friendly eye. They did not harm him, he was too large and strong, and when a dingo pack shot forward in a hunt for prey, their actions even excited him.

At five years of age Jago was a magnificent animal. His full growth and strength had been reached, his adaptation to the wild life was complete, and his body was rock hard. Little fat was visible over the rolling muscles and he had the thick, iron neck of the stallion, curved and arched with his intelligent head proud and even a trifle arrogant. His steps at the trot and canter were swinging and brisk with his red tail fluttering like a flag in the high breeze.

He was that truly magnificent animal seen by few people: the wild horse in his glory.

CHAPTER EIGHT

Capture !

B UT unknown to Jago, he had been seen.

Only one type of man could have the skill to see, creep up and observe, then depart as silently as he came without Jago knowing. The aborigine tracker saw the red horse late one afternoon. He was mounted but had left his horse ground-tied while he tracked across the ground. He was not looking for anything special but following his usual practice of occasionally riding far out into the bush and living partly wild like his fellow tribesmen who scorned the white man's civilization.

He was employed, amongst other things, as a tracker for the police but though he lived with the white man he had not entirely cut himself off from his fellows who went walkabout or lived in roaming tribes.

He was a very crafty man and when he saw the great red horse standing silently under the shade of a tree he made no sound but stared in admiration. He had never seen such a magnificent animal and he knew only too well how valuable he must be. He knew nothing of Jago's reputation for he had never heard of the racehorse turned rodeo jumper who had broken to freedom. All he knew was that here was a wonderful horse worth untold wealth to the man who could capture him.

The black man stared long and hard at the red horse, taking in every minute detail of the muscles, the body and stance, the alert head, the general supreme being of the horse.

He withdrew as silently as he had come, then sinking on his haunches he started thinking. If he obtained help from his fellows they would expect to share the value of the catch. Jegoda liked the white man's money far too much to want to share it and he resolved to capture the horse himself.

He was a first-class horseman, he had ample time to formulate his plans, and he had incredible patience.

For three weeks he watched the horse. Always approaching downwind, his footsteps absolutely silent, with his native cunning he took advantage of every piece of cover. He could stand for hours, dead still, in one position, the only sign of life in his nostrils and his slightly heaving chest. Not for nothing was he a tracker for the police. He could follow a trail which was invisible to a white man, even to one who was bush born and reared, and he was cleverer and more intelligent than many others of his kind.

Jago never knew he was being watched. During those three weeks he stayed in the locality of a water hole. There was, for once, ample feed and he was loath to leave such a place. The sun was not too hot at this time of the year and after all his wandering he was happy to stay in one spot.

He started forming habits. At a certain time of the day he would come down to drink, at another time he would eat; his rest was taken while the sun was in a certain position. He was always highly alert, but he had not been in the bush long enough to be able to beat such a highly skilled black tracker.

His watering place was down in a shallow dip and one slope was well covered with rocks which made a perfect hiding place. It was from here that his capture was planned.

Jegoda's plans were thorough and painstaking in their precision. The tracker knew that with a wild horse he would only ever have one chance. He tested his rope for flaws, he checked his saddle and rested his horse, and again and again went over his plan, trying to put himself in the horse's position. If he threw the rope from just there, what would the horse try to do?

He had kept his secret carefully. No-one knew where he went in the bush and no-one was particularly concerned. He was too skilled a person to die of thirst or get lost. He was an aborigine, supreme over the clumsy white man.

When he was thoroughly satisfied that every little detail had been considered, he picked his day. He had observed that the red horse came for water in the morning and late afternoon while between times he roamed around the vicinity feeding.

The tracker approached at midday. The very slight breeze was just right and he knew it would not change direction. He had muffled his own horse's hooves and left him tied a little distance away while he selected his hiding place.

Down between two rocks he would be quite invisible but, more valuable still, one rock had a sharp point where over the years the wind and weather had worn the softer rock away leaving just a protruding pinnacle of hard stone. It was around this he was going to anchor his rope to hold the horse while he fetched his own mount.

The tracker reached his hiding place, crawling in absolute silence, a few inches at a time, never hurrying, carefully removing every tiny obstacle in his path which might cause a noise under his body weight—two pebbles which could click together, a brittle twig which might snap, some grass fronds which could brush and whisper together; small sounds indiscernible to a white man but loud enongh to penetrate the ears of a an alert wild horse.

Once in his position the tracker sank down to wait. The sun beat down overhead but he crouched quite motionless, merging into the rocks with the rope coiled patiently in one hand.

Jago took his time eating and as the sun started sliding away to end another day he turned and slowly walked down for his evening drink. He did not hurry and his walk was almost lazy but he was highly alert. His ears were never still as they absorbed and classified all the bush sounds. The large nostrils were continually flaring and the eyes roamed to right and left, backward and forward, as with any wild animal coming down to drink water, for at this time they are most vulnerable to attack.

Jago reached the thick, black mud over which he had to cross to drink from the small pool underneath a large stone. With delicate steps he crossed the mud then stood by the water, looking all around. For five minutes he stood, then, satisfied he was quite alone, lowered his head and drank greedily.

The tracker moved with infinite care, flexing his muscles gradually to remove any kinks from the long wait. He rose in slow motion, his body movements beautifully controlled, and as he rose, the rope was ready in his hand. He knew he would have about five seconds and no more. As soon as the horse saw him, he would lift his head, stare for those five seconds, then whip aside in shock. Once that happened, the chance would be lost. He had to throw his rope while the horse stared in surprise, and anchor it before he plunged away.

Jago sensed the man before he saw him. He stopped sucking at the water while his ears moved in all directions, then quickly he lifted his head as the man rose above him. His nostrils inhaled the dreaded scent as the rope was already hurtling down, and he swung to the left, away from the trap.

But he was far too late. The rope had landed around his neck

He crouched quite motionless, merging into the rocks.

and was already tightening as he plunged against it. He felt the old familiar cutting and he braked, turned, and without a pause went towards the ambusher, ready to fight and die for his precious freedom.

The tracker had chosen his place too well, though. He had made his cast accurately, snubbed the rope around the rock, and dropped down out of sight.

Jago flung himself forward, his feet scrabbling to find a foothold but the slope was too steep and slippery with shale for a horse to climb. A goat would have managed it but Jago was helpless. He tried again and again as his temper flared, then slithering backward for the third time he halted and eyed the taut rope.

Rearing he struck at it with his feet but the rope was new and strong. He snapped with his teeth but the tracker threw a stone which distracted him. Jago tried another charge, his rage boiling, but the man was safely out of reach. Again and again he charged, his movements wild and exhausting, before he understood that he could never reach the man from this position.

Jago fumed and half reared in fury. To be caught after so much freedom! He screeched a warning, daring the man to come near, but the tracker was not such a fool. He had already gone for his own horse.

Once mounted again, he turned and rode back to the rock, edging his horse nearer and nearer, then he dismounted and watched the furious animal below. He had to transfer the rope to his saddle and drag the wild horse back with him. That was his plan, and it was a good one because most wild horses would have kept at the end of the rope, as far as possible from the terrible man scent. Jago, however, was no ordinary horse. He had had to work and fight for his freedom; it was not going to be taken from him now.

For a moment he stopped fighting and watched the man, his ears back, his hate only too obvious, his senses alert for the slightest opportunity which might be given to him. He saw the man transfer the rope to the pommel of his saddle but his short rush was checked because of the ground. His chance would surely come because he had to be taken out into the open some time, and away from the rocks.

The tracker also knew this. He intended riding his horse along the lip of the rocks, then, once down on the flat land, drag the wild horse behind. He felt no danger, he had his stock-whip and his own mount was strong and well trained to keeping a tension on the rope. Also, a horse with a rope cutting into his windpipe cannot win a tug-of-war against another horse with the rope around the saddle horn.

To start with the plan worked beautifully and the tracker was grinning to himself as he dragged the wild horse out into the open. He took his long, cutting whip in his right hand, holding the reins in his left, and guiding his mount with his legs. It had been so simple; all he had to do now was drag the horse back into the town. How everyone would stare when he came in with such a prize!

Poor, unfortunate black man, he had no idea that behind him he was dragging enough man-hate to explode a ton of dynamite. The first thing he knew, denoting all was not well, was the pounding of hoof-beats in his rear.

He turned swiftly in the saddle, his eyes opening wide in shock. The great red horse was hurtling straight for him, ears back, jaws open, evil shrieking from every red hair.

Never before had the tracker known a horse attack from the

end of a rope but swinging he lifted his whip and prepared to thrash the horse into submission.

The whip cracked in Jago's face but he never heard it. All he wanted to do was get at the man who had dared to capture him. The whip cracked again, this time the end of the lash biting into his breast, but he felt nothing. His rage was too hot, he was beyond physical pain.

Then Jago was on the rider. For a fraction of a second he was looking at the man's rolling eyes, his horror, his pitiful attempts to evade the teeth, then the red body had crashed broadside into his mount and his horse went down, struggling and whinnying in terror.

Jago was everywhere at once. He slashed at the fallen horse, one strong hoof leaving a red furrow as the shoulder skin split open, then he turned for the man.

The tracker had scrambled from beneath the saddle and had run aside to face the red devil with his only defence, the long whip.

Jago snorted, and without any battle preliminaries, charged straight for the black man. The whip crashed across his face and bit into his body but nothing could stop him now. He reared high, towering over the terrified tracker, then struck with both feet. A brisk, rattling tattoo and the black man crumpled, already dead, under the blows. But this did not satisfy the furious Jago. He reared again and again, to drop down and pound the lifeless hulk into a bloody smear in the dust. It took him five minutes to realize that no more harm would come to him from this man. Only then did Jago turn his attention to the horse.

The heavy fall had burst the saddle girth and the stock-horse, frantically scrambling erect again, had found he was not tied or controlled by the man. He had turned tail and fled without pause or hesitation.

Jago bounced after him but was brought up short. The rope was still firmly tied to the saddle pommel and he was dragging everything at his heels. So he turned his fury upon the leather, plunging and kicking until the rope broke under the strain and he was free again except for the remnant around his neck.

Once the tension was removed the rope started loosening around Jago's neck as he flexed his muscles. On lowering his head to sniff at the bloody mess of flesh and bones in the dust, it slipped around his ears. Jago shook his head, twitched his ears, and the loop dropped neatly on to the ground. This too was attacked with hooves and teeth until it was left a frayed, tattered fragment beside the tracker's body.

Still Jago stayed by the dead body of his enemy. The black man whom he had killed represented all men from whom he had suffered so much in the past and Jago's killer instinct was seething.

He circled the body, screeching, challenging it to rise and fight again, unwilling to leave while his hate and rage bubbled beneath the surface of his skin. For many months he had nursed the will to kill a man; now he had succeeded, the power and glory were like a drug. He exulted and screamed his victory for all to hear.

He was Jago, the supreme, the killer, the champion! And once again he reared, his head raised in triumph as the blood-smell thrust into his nostrils. Never before had he felt such power, never before had he enjoyed such a victory. Life would never be the same again because there was nothing he now feared. Man was the easiest creature in the world to kill when he did not have the loud shooting stick and the rope, the harness that caused pain. For the last time he reared and pounded the tattered thing then scornfully kicked it apart with his hind legs.

Gradually his temper dropped and the blood-smell became distasteful to his nostrils so, turning, he trotted away, his bouncing steps proclaiming his victory for all the bush to see. He had his drink at the water-hole and stared once more at the body; then he turned and left.

He had enough sense to realize that other men would come searching and they might have the shooting sticks. His departure was not the flight of fear but the more leisurely progress of a horse who has at last succeeded in an accomplishment.

Jago struck out into fresh territory, leaving behind a mystery which puzzled men for many months. They came and found the tracker's body, they read the signs of a fight with a horse but they were none the wiser. The tracker had been without peer in his work, his bush lore was unique. What kind of horse had killed him—and where was he? The stockmen ranged far and wide, hunting for the killer, seeking his tracks, their rifles at the alert, but Jago had long since learned to travel over hard ground and hide his progress. In the end, the tracker's death was just another bush mystery and it was only many years later, when the tales of a great red horse began circulating, that one or two men thought and wondered: could it have been this horse? Was it possible?

Jago headed further out into the Northern Territory, leaving the water-hole far behind, never to be visited again. His never-ending quest now was for companionship from his own kind.

He ranged far and wide, heading deeper and deeper into wild

open country. From time to time he saw a boundary rider from some large cattle station checking the wire fences, but Jago avoided men now. He had satisfied his killer urge, he had taken his revenge and he knew that such white men always carried the dreaded shooting stick. Even he, the great Jago, dare not tackle such a combination, so wherever he came across some lonely wire fence, he turned away. Fences meant men and shooting sticks and acute danger.

The months passed. The hot sun beat down, the country rolled forever onward with plains and hills, slopes and dried-up gulleys, all in browns and fawns, covered everywhere with dust. Rain was scarce. Sometimes it fell but more often the weather failed and Jago often passed piles of bleached bones where the white men's cattle had died in the agony of thirst.

Jago sometimes failed to find water himself but he had become so hard and tough that he did not need to drink as much as the domesticated animal. He had learned to obtain a certain amount of moisture from what he ate, and when he did find water, he drank and drank, filling his system to excess.

He always found food too though it varied in quality and quantity, so although at times he was hungry he never actually starved. Always however, over and above these prime considerations of hunger and thirst, Jago was searching for companionship. He had been alone far too long. The yearning to play and squeal and dance with other wild horses was growing stronger every day and, unknown to him, he was slowly heading in the direction where brumbies lived. These were the large herds of wild horses, brought into Australia by the early settlers, which had escaped, run free and wild, and learned to live off the land.

Every night and morning Jago positioned himself on the

highest point of land and stood patiently scanning, searching, and scenting for other horses.

He now knew every bush scent and sound. Nothing was strange to him, he had met or seen everything that mattered, everything except the one thing his heart cried out for.

Now and again, he would whinny over the air and stand in patient silence, straining to catch some response; but none came, and disappointed he would descend to eat, drink, or rest.

He was patient, however, and his direction was true. If he had veered off to right or left he would have missed the herd but the cluster of hills, the absolute wildness of the land ahead, drew him like a magnet. This was to be explored and learned and Jago knew that in such remote areas men were practically unknown. They had no cause or reason to ride here, their strange cattle could not live. It was the perfect haven and hiding-place for the wild horse.

The hills were mottled in various shades of brown and fawn with trees sprinkled here and there. As he approached Jago smelt water and his ears pricked. He was feeling thirsty, he had not drunk since morning, and he had travelled a long way.

He walked more quickly, following the smell, relishing in advance the taste of cool, wet liquid sliding down his dusty throat. Life was very good, and if ample feed was there too, he could rest a few days.

But Jago was now extremely cautious on approaching any watering place. He never went straight up but approached in a curving circle, testing the air all around for hidden enemies. Never again would any man catch him from a hidden ambush. Jago had learned his lesson too well.

He completed a silent walk around the water, satisfied

himself it was free from the hated man-scent, then turning to go in and drink, he halted in shock.

The fresh, newly-made scent smacked his nostrils and he inhaled in delight.

Horses—and many of them!

CHAPTER NINE

Royal Battle

J AGO was so wildly excited that he did not know what to
do first. Should he shout his presence? Should he make a
cautious approach and spy out the land or would it perhaps
be wiser to have his drink first?

He was torn apart by the fierce emotions in his heart and the
pain from his thirsty body and he stood for many minutes in
hopeless indecision. After so long a solitary life he craved
companionship as much as his throat cried out for water to
remove the fine dust particles. His legs were weary after his
long trek but still he stood, rooted to one spot, wavering and
hesitating as joy chased through his body.

At last he decided and made his slow approach to the water.
Bodily urges were, at this stage, stronger than mental ones. He
knew horses were around somewhere, he could find them
once his thirst has been quenched.

He drank with quick impatience, satisfying the needs of his
body, and to refresh himself he rolled, plastering the thick mud
over his coat. Then scrambling erect, he stood and shook
himself.

The sun had started its descent and in another hour or so it
would be night. Jago was not too hungry; all he wanted to do
was to find the horse herd.

He swung his head low, assimilating the gorgeous scents,
then tracking after them, he walked forward. He did not scream
his approach, he was now far too cautious, and as the horse

scent became even stronger in his nostrils he halted, lifting his head up, feeling for the breeze. Turning aside, he swung in a large circle, making his approach downwind where he could see and not be seen.

He broke into a trot, his whole gait joyful and sprightly, but when he knew he was nearing the herd, he slowed right down to a careful walk. He put his feet down as silently as any roaming cat and keeping to the already darkening shadows he drew nearer to the slope.

It was long and gradual but he favoured a high position from where he would have a grand viewpoint. At the top of the slope half a dozen gum trees clustered together and it was under these, in their shadow, that Jago halted, stood, and surveyed the scene below.

His heart was pounding with excitement and joy at the realization that there below were members of his own kind. There was the companionship for which he had yearned all those lonely, wandering months. Horses of all shapes and colours, big ones, small ones, mares and foals, all busily eating, pulling and tearing at the coarse grass.

The shallow valley in which they ate was sheltered on three sides and on the fourth was open to the plains. The water-hole was very large indeed which explained the herds being there, and the few trees which grew on the valley floor and partially up the hill slopes were ideal for shade during the noonday heat. It was a perfect place for a herd of wild horses. They had the open exit for wandering upon the plains, and the three slopes of the hills made the valley snug. A sentinel, perched high upon a rocky pinnacle, would have a perfect view of the valley, making a surprise approach difficult.

In fact, silent as Jago's approach had been, he was already

known to be there. The enormous grey stallion, leader of the herd, had become aware of the stranger's presence two minutes ago and he stood, testing the scent, wondering, trying to locate the exact spot in the darkness.

The moon broke free of the clouds and Jago moved slowly from the trees and stood exposed to open view. He flung up his head, and blared a whinny of introduction and friendship.

Every head in the valley lifted, every animal turned to face the sound, and curious nickers arose from many throats. A strange horse on the hillside! The nickers sounded again, interested and a little flirtatious, wanting to know more details.

Jago stood still, his heart beating with more vigour as their sounds rose up to him in greeting. A horse does not know tears—to weep is the prerogative of man—but if Jago could have wept, he would have done so then, his heart was bursting with such great happiness.

The grey stallion flashed his ears backward and tossed his head while he weighed up the situation. His position was superior in height to that of Jago and he had a clear track down to the valley floor.

He knew that another stallion was wishing to enter his domain and, although the calls had been full of friendship, the grey stallion knew no such emotion. He was all horse. The mares and foals below belonged to him and him alone. He was their guardian, their soldier, their teacher, and their mate. The small foals were beneath his notice, only to be protected or punished if they did something stupid. More attention was paid to the yearlings and especially the yearling colts. Upon these he kept a watchful eye. The two-year-old male horses he hated and ruthlessly drove from his domain. If they went quietly, they lived. If they objected and were foolish enough to try and challenge for the herd leadership, then he killed them without compunction. No male horse over two years of age was allowed anywhere near the mares and fillies.

And over there was an intruder, a male and adult. The grey's eyes blazed with rage at this impertinence and turning he started to wend his way down the track to the valley below. He did not hurry. He had fought many battles and he had learned to conserve his energy for the fight alone.

The grey was neither very young nor very old. He was a big horse, in his prime. Bush born and bred, he only knew man the enemy from sight in the outback. No rope had ever encircled his neck, no saddle had been clamped on his back. He was all horse and all wild.

The stallion broke into a trot on the valley floor and slowly circled his mares and foals, bunching them together. Displaying his ownership and authority, he was making it perfectly plain to the red stranger that the herd was his.

Jago stood and watched in silence. He had never seen a stallion round up his mares before but he did not have to be told what was going on. This was a display of ownership and for his benefit alone. These are mine, it said; if you are wise, you will go. This land is mine, this water is mine, this feed is mine! You are the trespasser! Go—if you want to continue living!

Jago's feelings were mixed. His desire for companionship burned with as fierce a flame as had his longing for freedom so long ago, but, although untaught by any wild dam, Jago knew the law. It had been handed down to him as had his alert instinct, his will to live, his desire to fight for what he wanted.

The grey horse was behaving in a perfectly correct manner

in staking claim to his possessions. That was the law. It was also the law that if Jago stayed, he would be forced to fight, and when two stallions fight there is only one more law to understand—that of live or die. There is rarely any surrender and flight is rather to be despised—in front of interested mares.

Jago was not looking for a fight but if he turned and left now —what remained? Another life of lonely wandering until he found a second brumby herd? If he did, the result would only be the same. Every herd has its jealous leader stallion.

Jago had no intention of leaving. Apart from the fact that he was keen to introduce himself with squeals and nips to these wonderful new-found friends, he was not the type to turn from a threat.

There was also another factor. Jago too was a stallion. He had never had a mate, he had been lonely too long; it was only right that he, in his turn, should propagate his kind. But as amongst all wild animals, a mate must be courted, and attracted, and fought for. The female in the wild must be won in open combat. In every bird and animal species, this is the strongest and oldest law of all; it is also the one which commands the most respect.

As Jago stared down at the moving grey stallion his emotions were changing. The warm friendship was being pushed down for the hard challenge of the stallion, seeking mates and a territory of his own. The time had come to announce his intention to the mares and the grey stallion.

Jago reared high into the air, silhouetted against the trees in the moon's rays. He opened his jaws and screeched forth his challenge, his tone harsh and brassy. For the first time in his life, he screamed the universal challenge of one stallion to another.

Jago dropped and stared down at the grey. The stallion reared back, replying in kind, and so the duel was announced, the place fixed, the witnesses informed.

Spinning on his hocks, Jago majestically turned to descend to lower ground. The defender had the choice of position and he stood, his grey body well in front of the clustered mares and foals. Many eyes were turned upon the red horse as he came down to battle for the right to live as a stallion.

The mares shivered in excitement. Was this to be their new lord? The foals cringed in terror at their dams' sides. What was going to happen now? The yearlings, already feeling their own blood stir, stared in concentration, avid to watch and learn for when their turn came.

Jago halted six yards from the grey stallion and both animals stared at each other with burning eyes. For once, Jago was in no hurry to fling himself into battle without the preliminaries. The rules must be obeyed; this was not a fight against a mere man or against some poor stock-horse. This was a matter of life or death before the keenest witnesses in the world—mares!

Both stallions felt affinity for each other. Both were strong horses, leaders in their own right. Each knew every individual law of the wild. Before the contest started, they sized each other up; they compared muscles, height, weight, and reach, length of striking hoof, depth of biting teeth, stamina, and power of determination.

They were sharply contrasted, the grey and the red coats shining under the moon. They stood like gladiators in a Roman amphitheatre. Blood was going to flow and one must die. The crown of royalty was at stake because they were, both of them, of ancient royal lineage.

Jago's aristocratic breeding went back through his Australian ancestors to the long line of proud English thoroughbreds which started, over two centuries ago, with the importation into England of the three foundation Arabian sires: the Darley Arabian, the Godolphin Arabian, and the Byerley Turk. His indeed was the blood of royalty.

Oddly enough, the grey stallion too had proud ancestors. His had first broken loose from the early settlers to roam wild in the great new continent of Australia, and like all his ancestors the grey stallion showed his good blood with his flaring Arabian nostrils, his delicate legs, and his curving nose.

This was to be no fight between common, cold-blooded horses, but a genuine battle royal.

It was time now for the preliminaries and both horses half reared, squealing threats to each other: what they were going to do, how brave and mighty they were, how foolish and weak was the other. They snapped their legs down, sending the dust spurting upwards as they performed their war dance, then knowing their audience was satisfied they prepared for the real matter at hand—the actual battle.

They charged together, crashed and reared high, screaming their horrible threats as red and grey heads darted backward and forward searching for the great artery, while with their front legs they struck and flailed, each tearing the other's skin.

The blood flowed, staining and spreading, but neither horse felt pain. Their blood was too hot, their nerves too tense and alert, their muscles too set in iron bands.

They rose again and this time jaws met on flesh, teeth sank into skin and were pulled clear. Their hocks strained under the weight of their respective bodies and Jago, tiring quickly of this apparent stalemate, decided to change his battle tactics. He dropped down, quickly spun on his hocks, and kicked hard

They charged together, crashed and reared high

with both hind legs. The blows landed full and square on the grey's ribs but the stallion scorned to flinch. He too turned and lashed out, his hooves tearing strips of skin from Jago's bunched quarters.

They stood back to back now, and rained blows on each other, neither missing, each doing damage; then as one they turned and faced each other again and, half rearing, boxed with their forelegs. The blows were swift, the rock-sharpened hooves as deadly as butchers' knives, and both stallions soon had long open cuts on their shoulders and breasts.

Jago flung himself forward, right on top of the striking hooves, ignoring the damage they were doing as he strained to sink his teeth in the great pulsing vein. He was pushing the grey stallion backward while his teeth were stabbing and tearing, punishing, but each time just missing the artery.

As they fought, their neck muscles flexed, protecting the great life-giving blood, and once again they reared high, each trying to outstand the other. Being of equal height, however, this movement also was a stalemate.

They dropped down and started another round of kicking. Tail to tail, they lashed and hurled blows at each other's bloody body, grunting and squealing with effort and rage. The dust rose in a cloud, almost covering their movements, until they broke through on to fresh ground.

By this time the grey horse was covered in blood and looked in worse condition than he really was, owing to the colour of his coat; Jago too was bleeding profusely though this was to some extent disguised by his colouring.

The battle raged on and the mares never took their eyes off the fighters.

For ten minutes they hurled themselves at each other with

hoof and tush but neither gave ground. They whirled around, fastened on to each other, never still for a second, writhing as skin and muscles were severed and more blood flowed.

They fought in silence now. Each horse realized that this was not just another ordinary fight. His opponent was of a different mould, the victor would have to work hard to win.

Tearing apart they broke away for two paces, turned, then charged at each other, the hocks driving the great bodies forward on a collision course. They met with a mighty bang which echoed all over the valley and each slightly winded himself but Jago was a fraction quicker to recover.

The grey stallion was a good fighter but he did not have Jago's terrific drive. He had not been through quite such a hard school of living and he lacked Jago's astonishing speed.

In a second, the red horse renewed his attack with seemingly fresh vigour, just as if what had gone before was a mere try-out of strength. The red head and neck were everywhere, biting and tearing, while the red legs with the razor-sharp front hooves drummed a ceaseless tattoo against the grey's body.

Jago flung himself into his very top gear and increased his speed and pressure still more, until quite suddenly the grey found—to his horror—that he was having to give ground. His grey hocks strained to hold their position but the hooves started slipping as the red body pushed and shoved, teeth and legs never ceasing their action.

The grey felt one hind leg shaking under the strain and he struggled to retain his upright stance. To go down before this wild, red devil would be the end.

Jago sensed his opponent's weakening and he pushed forward harder; he gripped the grey mane with his teeth, lodged his forelegs around the grey shoulders, and silently wrestled, trying to overturn the grey.

The grey felt the awful pressure, the terrible, driving strength, the weakening of his hind legs, the slithering of the one hoof. He was falling, he was—

The grey slithered and fell in a tangled heap of red and grey legs. Jago dragged himself erect, reared high, and towered over his opponent's head which lifted and looked up at him.

The grey's eyes were wide open as he stared at death. His ears were pricked forward acknowledging his defeat, his voice uttered no sound, no cry for mercy. From the depths of his heart and will he flung a last vision into his eyes.

High above him, poised for the coup-de-grâce, Jago's eyes bored down into the grey's. Their gaze met and locked as the spirit, the communication and will of mutual stallionship, flowed between them.

I, who am about to die, salute you, said the grey's spirit. Take care of these mares. They are fine mares, they breed good foals. This land, my Kingdom, I bequeath to you. This bush, this feed, this water, I hand to you in trust and stallion spirit, to have and to hold, from this moment forward.

The red head stared down. The two pairs of eyes met and Jago's spirit answered: I take your crown, I take your mares and foals, I take your land and water, I, Jago the great and magnificent, I take your rôle. I will guard your mares and fight and protect this trust until I too become but dust under the dingoes' paws. I, Jago the king, take your crown and throne. I give you one thing only—I herewith give you death!

The hooves descended, striking square and true. The grey's bones crunched, split apart and the artery severed at last. As the grey's eyes flickered for the last time he held the red eyes to his trust and promise, to his rôle of royal dictate, then slowly they glazed and the grey stallion was dead.

Jago turned, half reared before his witnesses, and screamed forth his proclamation: The king is dead! I am the king!

The mares and fillies whinnied and screeched back: The king is dead! You are the king!

Jago reared high again, stretching right up at the moon, demonstrating his might, his greatness, his masculinity, then braying forth, he screamed over the still night air.

The dingoes and possums, the roosting birds and kangaroos, all the inhabitants of the bush, stopped what they were doing and listened to the battle cry. Their silence was a token of their acknowledgement of the crowning and coronation of the new king.

Jago stamped with his front hoof, pawing and demonstrating, then turning again, he cantered wildly around the corpse of his opponent. His head was low, snaking over the ground, undulating to right and left; then back he came to stand in front of the mares.

Another screaming rear, another final proclamation, and he stepped forward to claim his inheritance. The mares parted for his royal progress and as he walked through them they extended their heads and inhaled his scent. They were giddy with excitement and awe. The foals cringed away from this magnificent personage and the yearling colts stared with frightened eyes at such royalty.

Jago's crown was his aura. His throne was this land, his subjects were all around. He had lived through many great moments but none, either before or ever again, would be like this. The coronation of a stallion comes but once in his lifetime. His other battles are in defence of his kingdom.

Jago broke through the whinnying and nickering mares, pushed himself into a snappy trot and circled his harem, snaking his head up and down, to left and right. He completed his circle and did another, this time at a brisk canter with his head high in pride and glory; then accelerating he flung himself into his racing gallop, bunching the mares in closer and closer, enforcing his will, bending their spirits to his.

Once he was sure they accepted him he set himself at their head, screamed a command, and broke forward in a trot. The herd passively followed.

The trot became a canter and the canter flowed into a gallop. The herd's excitement rose and the mares hurled themselves after their lord and master. Colourful heads, tails switching, manes flowing, their hooves rattled over the ground making a rumble as of thunder. The dust rose in a huge cloud, like the warning of a bush fire, the valley echoed to their passing and all other wild animals hastily got out of their path. This king would stop for nothing!

And so the great horse Jago came into his birthright. The blood which nature had fused to make him different from his contemporaries would flow on and on now, for ever and ever, through the mares that followed at his tail.

Jago needed no tuition in herd management. All the knowledge and bush-lore necessary he had been slowly acquiring over months and years. All the strength and will had been born in him, and, like steel, had been tempered in the flames of battle with men.

He had been born and come into being at man's dictate but nature had intervened and he himself had sought for, found, and then fought to win his natural inheritance.

No stallion was as wild and clever as Jago. No stallion knew

more about the bush than Jago. No stallion would protect his
mares and foals more zealously from thirst or hunger. Even in
the most bitter drought the red stallion would somehow find
water. In the hottest and cruellest weather every member of
the herd was guarded against all dangers. Even the most clever
and quick two-year-old colt gave way to him, and all over his
kingdom Jago left bleached bones. He had no mercy for any
male horse over one year. He fought many battles and became
supreme, he ruled his tightly-knit community with a hoof of
iron and no mare objected. That was as it should be. That was
the law.

The great red stallion was cunning and guile personified. His
dealings with men had taught him exactly what to expect,
when to move aside, when to trespass and steal. He was
superb because men had made him so.

There was no finer sight than that which greeted the eyes of
any stranger bold enough to approach the royal kingdom.
When the sun was setting in a fiery ball, dipping down towards
the horizon, he would see the world's most marvellous
spectacle—the great herd of wild horses thundering into the
valley to drink at the water hole. They would come in at the
gallop, led by the great red stallion, and two paces behind would
be his favourite mare with a red foal at foot. They would rumble
down between the slopes, making their own brand of thunder,
and the ground would shake under their passing. The herd
would gather around to drink, squabbling and picking at each
other with squeals and grunts, and not until every mare and
youngster had taken his and her share would the red stallion
slake his own thirst.

He would approach, in majestic grandeur bow his head,
drink his fill, turn to inspect his charges, then slowly, one

strong hoof moving in unison with its neighbour, he would climb the slopes of one of the hills.

High at the top of this hill is a rocky platform of shale and on one side a dead flat, smooth, white rock. This is the actual throne and it is here that a great horse takes his stand and guard over his charges. From here he can see the approach of any intruder no matter how big or small. From here every breath of wind reaches his nostrils to be analysed and classified before being stored in his brain. From here every tiny whisper of sound is filtered by the sharp ears before their message is passed on to the brain.

This great horse sleeps with one eye open, with both ears working, and with both nostrils at full flare. It is quite impossible to creep up on him unawares because he is Jago the great—and he knows everything.

CHAPTER TEN

The Legend

AUSTRALIA is a great land-mass straddling the area between longitudes 113° and 150° and between latitudes 10° and 39°. This huge continent soars to its highest point at Mount Kosciusko but most of the rest of the country is a vast plateau sprinkled with low hills, some forest, brown plains, and yellow desert.

It has been agreed that the Dutch ship *Duyfhen* first discovered the country in 1606 but it was Captain Cook, on April 20th, 1770, who sighted New Holland.

The first white people to live there landed in about 1778 but these people were convicts and their guards; the first real immigrants arrived in New South Wales in the year 1793. With the discovery of gold, the population increased at a great rate and the "Australian" was born; his ancestry was chiefly British.

The Australian aborigines had no chance at all against the superior white man; their stone-age way of life was powerless against the rifle and they gave ground rapidly before this invasion of white supremacy. In Tasmania they became quite extinct and in Australia herself the number of full-bloods diminished as the aborigines either went farther out into the bush or became to some extent integrated into the white man's way of life.

As the country thrived so did its folklore and legends. Writers and poets immortalized Australia in poetry and prose.

Rolf Boldrewood gave the reader Captain Starlight and his
famous horse Rainbow, while Adam Lindsay Gordon sketched
the bush in his famous ballad *"The Sick Stockrider"*.

Every Australian child knows of the notorious bush-ranger
Ned Kelly, just as he knows the legend of the faithful dog
sitting on his master's tucker box at Gundagai, waiting with
canine devotion for the dying master who never returned. And
as they know these stories so they gradually, child and man,
come to hear of another great legend.

It is the legend of a horse, a great red horse that ran a herd
of brumbies somewhere in the outback. As the legend grew,
passing from mouth to mouth, growing in the telling, it awoke
memories in certain men. It made them think and it made
them wonder.

It was an aborigine who started the story. He told it to his
tribesmen who in turn related it to their more civilized com-
rades and from there it drifted to the attention of the white
stockmen who run the great sheep and cattle stations. Slowly it
moved outwards to the cities, growing in strength and majesty.

The story told of a horse that was king in the outback. A
horse so gifted with cunning and guile, so endowed with
strength and intelligence, that no man could believe it until he
had seen.

This great red horse ran his herd just wherever he chose,
stealing, trespassing, and fighting the man or beast that dared to
stand in his path. So men went out to find this fabulous creature
to see if he really existed. But few caught more than a glimpse
of him because it was quite impossible to creep up on him in
the open; his eyes were too sharp, his ears too keen, his flaring
nostrils too alert. The faintest trace of man-danger threatening
his herd made him spring to the lead, and with rumbling

hooves the horses would vanish, like poinsettia leaves blown away in a sudden willy-willy. Red flames would vanish into the sun-burnt land. Where the horses went no man knew because in the direction the red horse headed there was only a hot wasteland in which nothing could live.

Even a helicopter failed. The great red horse's acute danger-sense had never met anything quite like it before but he knew a helicopter meant danger from man and by the time the pilot had allowed for the air currents as he dropped down from the hills, the herd had vanished. Turn his machine as he might, he never saw the herd again, and disbelieving his eyes, cursing at the desert mirage, he flew back to base, ridiculing the legend of the red horse.

But the legend grew and grew of this king of the outback with his great herd of mares and red foals, their colour as warm and bold as the embers from the stockmen's camp fires when, blowing on their billies of scalding tea, they talked and wondered.

Such a horse could not exist. The story was too fantastic to be true. It was just some wild, fanciful legend from aborigine history, they said, but on reflection, they paused and wondered again as they remembered a big red horse from the rodeos who, filled with hate, had suddenly vanished at the exact time of his death sentence.

Three other men remembered too—the crippled black aborigine Warrigan, the tall stockman Mike Colston, and the small, dapper racehorse trainer Peter Huston. Could it be—was it possible—did Jago live on? Was there really a herd of wild red horses somewhere out there? Or was it just black man's talk? No man ever knew for certain but deep in the hearts of all lay sympathy and respect for the great red horse if he did truly exist. They admired toughness, courage, and guts—and if Jago was alive and king then he must certainly have all three attributes—but could it be, was it really he, or was it just another bush legend?

Somewhere out there you might, if you are very lucky, find out for yourself. You must go up to Queensland, move west into the bush, take a bearing north, cross it with another to the west and press on yet again. If you are as cunning as a stalking dingo, as silent as a snake, as swift and bold as a hunting eagle, you might find out for yourself. But it will be a long trek, a hard one and a hot one. Make sure you take plenty of water with you but most of all take caution. If by chance you do stumble on the red horse do it with prudence and respect. Give the king his royal due and be prepared to flee if his wrath is high, for the great red horse hates all men. Of them he has no fear.

Why should he?

He is Jago, the supreme. King of the outback.